I0634205

Karen grew up in a small country town in north-eastern Victoria, Australia. She spent her childhood riding horses through beautiful scenery of eucalypts, lakes, and snow-capped mountains and her love of landscape deeply affects her writing. She worked in a range of educational settings and holds a Ph.D. and M.Ed. (Hons) in the areas of fantasy. She is particularly interested in the power of the hero's inner journey which she explores through Deep Fantasy. Karen has travelled extensively overseas but enjoys nothing more than camping in the Australian Outback. She lives in Melbourne and now writes full-time. You can find out more about Karen and her books on her website.

Connect with K.S. Nikakis

Amazon: https://www.amazon.com/author/ksnikakis
Twitter: https://twitter.com/KSNikakis
Facebook: www.facebook.com/ksnikakis
Goodreads: www.goodreads.com
Website: www.ksnikakis.com
Email: author@ksnikakis.com

WORKS BY K S NIKAKIS

Non Fiction

Journey: Seeking the Sacred, Spirit and Soul in the
Australian Wilderness

Fantasy Novels Series

Angel Caste series:
Angel Blood
Angel Breath
Angel Bone
Angel Bound
Angel Blessed
Angel Caste – Complete 5 Book Series

The Kira Chronicles trilogy:*
The Whisper of Leaves
The Song of the Silvercades
The Cry of the Marwing
remnant hard copies only

The Kira Chronicles series:
The Whisper of Leaves
The Silence of Stone
The Secrets of Stars
The Thunder of Hoofs
The Crying of Birds
The Music of Home
The Kira Chronicles – Complete 6 Book Series

Fantasy Novels

The Emerald Serpent
Heart Hunter
The Third Moon
Messenger
I Heard the Wolf Call My Name
Finalist - Best YA Novel Aurealis Awards, 2019

Fantasy Short Stories

The Gift
The Tale of Prince Anura
Dragon Sprite
Glass-Heart
Finalist – Best YA Short Story Aurealis Awards, 2019

THE THIRD MOON

Waking the future,
Dreaming the past...

K.S. NIKAKIS

First published by SOV Media Australia 2017

Publisher: SOV Media
Melbourne, Australia.

Cover by AS Nikakis: http://asnikakis.com
PsychoShadow/Shutterstock.com

National Library of Australia
Cataloguing-in-Publication entry:
Nikakis, Karen Simpson
The Third Moon
ISBN 978-0-6482652-5-2

For Denise and Alan Shearer

GLOSSARY

CPS - Compatible Planetary Systems – similar to Earth and so easy to settle

DEM – Designated Essential Materials – resources Earth identifies as valuable

IFNO – Indigenous First Nations Oceania – people identified as having occupied a particular sector of Earth (in this case Oceania) for thousands of years

IJ - Interstellar Judiciary – Earth's justice system administered in space

Space Corp – Company running Earth's Exploration and Settler programs

Independent Affiliates – Ships outside of Space Corp but carrying out Space Corp business

ILFII - Indigenous Life-Forms Intelligence Index – a way of measuring the intelligence of a planet's fauna

Mechs – Mechtechnicians – tradesmen charged with assembling and maintaining the Settlements

Satellites/Sats - planets claimed by Earth

SciCorp - Scientific Corporation for the Investigation and Preservation of Off-Earth Life

Forms – scientists charged with studying and recording fauna and flora on planets

Trads – ships operating outside Space Corp's control and often involved in black-trade

THE THIRD MOON

!

I used to think it began with the murder I committed but maybe that was just arrogance and I am hoping my arrogance was swept away along with everything else on that fateful day. Hope might be arrogant too, I do not know. Lirra says it is human to hope but I do not even know what it means to be human anymore. I have started to believe that Imago has changed us, that we are something else, not like the flightborn yet but no longer like those on Earth.

Then again, who knows what those on Earth are like now? Do they still murder? Still hope? Still even exist? Whatever is happening on that far away planet, there were dozens of murders here on Imago before mine, all like drops of water in an immense wave that none of us saw coming.

But I am getting ahead of myself. Years before any of this took place, Planet XF-2010BX1 became Earth Satellite Imago, or the Sat or just Imago. Station One was established and the Scientific Corporation for the Investigation and Preservation of Off-Earth Life Forms, otherwise known as SciCorp, began our work.

Our job was to study the stars and rocks and soil, the forests and grasses, the creatures that crawled and ran and swam and flew, and to send off our records and reports to Earth, long after Earth stopped sending anything back.

And like all the Sats Earth claimed, we needed the Mechs to assemble the pods and what the pods contained, to make and mend whatever was missing, and to keep the whole thing ticking over so that we could carry out our work.

SciCorp and the Mechs arrived on the same Settler Ships but we were always a different species. When SciCorp looked at the Striate Forests, we saw an ancient and unchanging organism while the Mechs saw wood; and when SciCorp looked at the maggots, we saw Imago's prime sentient fauna, while the Mechs saw the opioid arrash in its purest form. SciCorp and the Mechs were on Imago for different reasons but when the Mechs got their hands on the arrash, they decided their reasons far out-weighed ours.

The Fighting was never going to be equal and, in the end, the SciCorp survivors were grateful to trade certain death at Station One for uncertain survival in the Iron Ranges. But even as a boy, I was never grateful, and my anger grew over the years until it was as deep as the stinking detritus of the Striate Forests and, like the detritus, needed only a single spark to ignite it. And that spark came on the day I turned down the tunnels towards Sapphire Bay and met a Mech coming up.

I was seventeen and can hardly remember why I headed down towards the glittering ocean instead of up deeper into the Iron Ranges, except that Sapphire Bay had always drawn me. I had grown up trying to remember what it had been like to walk along its sandy beaches, to swim in its warm waters, to eat fish that were sweet and clean.

I dreamed of what it would have been like had we won the Fighting instead of the Mechs, if we had access to everything the Settler Ship delivered in its sealed metal pods and the Mechs been forced to grub out a living in the Iron Ranges. But even as a boy I knew that a SciCorp victory had never been possible.

I can still see the Mech I met in the tunnel: his fair curly hair, his blue eyes and his shock as he crashed through the floor above and somehow landed on his feet right in front of me. The Mechs did not understand the Iron Ranges or the layers of matted leaves, branches and barkfall that formed multi-storeyed tunnels or maggot-runs through the forest floor. SciCorp investigated them early in Station One's life and knew that in places they were up to ten layers deep.

SciCorp also knew that no two tunnels were the same. Some floors were so thin they gave way under a cho-melon, while others did not care if a rast trunk fell on them. There were places too where weaknesses in the tunnel floors aligned to form shafts.

The Mech was lucky he had not fallen into one of those, or he would have kept on crashing through floor after floor, ending up in some dark hole with no way out. But he was also unlucky.

There was enough light from the hole he made for me to see his hand lunge for his weapon but I had already launched into the air, my shoulder aimed at his midriff. The force threw him backwards and smashed the air from his lungs, exactly as I practised with Ewan. The trouble was, I had never practised what came next.

When I brooded at night amongst the tors above Haven, I imagined dispatching my Mech enemies with a clean sweep of a matra blade, but as I pinned the Mech to the tunnel floor, I did not have my blade with me, in fact, I did not even have a rock.

The Mech bucked under me and, as he all but threw me off, I did the only thing possible: I grabbed him by the neck and squeezed. I can still feel the way his windpipe bent, hear the wheeze of his breath, see the spit and blood that spewed from his mouth.

He fought like a madman and I hung on like one. His nails raked my face but he could not reach his weapon and in the end his arms were as limp as him. It was a long time before I unclenched my hands and days before they stopped aching.

When I had breath enough, I dragged him down the tunnel until I found the tell-tale rusty bloom of fal-lichen. I was not stupid enough to go any closer, just rolled the Mech the last of the way until the floor collapsed. I counted the crashes as he plunged through the layers and reached nine before the racket stopped.

He had reached the deepest parts of the tunnels where even the maggots did not go, but there were plenty of things down there to welcome him.

Shadcats ate anything dead or living and grey worms cleared up what the shadcats left behind. And then there were the dry-slimes. They would take care of his bones and hair and even his clothing would slide into their glutinous bellies, to be dissolved and later expelled as crad: pellets of acid excrement.

The crashing had scarcely stopped before I ran back up the tunnel, driven by an irrational fear other Mechs knew what I had done and were in hot pursuit, but after a while, my heightened senses told me no one followed and I slowed.

There was no fal-lichen heralding shafts, just lumen-lichen to light the way and the purplish smudge of ceili-lichen that told me maggots had passed this way before.

I reached the exit that would have tipped me out near Haven but kept on going. My cheeks stung from the Mech's nails and I needed to wash the scratches and give them time to heal. I also needed to concoct a story of how I had acquired them.

I considered throwing myself into a stand of spine bush but when I found a tunnel exit early the next morning, I was in the Striate Forests, and nothing grew there but striate.

It was too soon to turn back and I went on, weaving between the ancient trunks, and eventually came out into a narrow valley. I was a lot higher in the Ranges than I usually roamed but I sensed I had been here before and, when I saw the cleft-peak ahead, I knew I was right.

I had been fourteen on my first visit and my anger and resentment at its height. I had stormed away from Haven after some argument with Hans and struggled up through the striate and on past where I now stood.

Ahead the valley tapered into a gorge so narrow you could touch the moss-covered walls on either side with your out-stretched hands and a stream wound its way down between stones and heaps of shattered translucent shells. The gorge widened again towards the end, just below the peak and there it was pocked with dozens of openings, some too small for even a child to crawl into and others big enough to enter without stooping.

Having orientated myself, I went on over the stony ground and through the shadowy dankness of the gorge and there were the caves, exactly as I remembered them. But the shells looked different to my older eyes, more like pieces of broken glass than the shells Lirra and I had collected along the shores of Sapphire Bay.

The caves were the sort of thing that would have drawn a fourteen-year-old boy desperate to prove something, anything about himself, but I had not gone into them then and I did not go into them now.

I would have struggled to explain why even to Lirra, but somehow in my head they had become mixed up with my mother's stories about the Dreaming. She had told me the Dreaming spirits created special sacred places that belonged only to men and special sacred places that belonged only to women, and that a man must never intrude into a woman's sacred place or a woman into a man's.

To my fourteen-year-old self, the ragged collection of holes had taken on the aura of the sacred places of the Dreaming and, despite being three years older, the sense they were closed to me remained strong, and again I let them be.

4

2

I stayed near the caves for five days. I bathed my face in the stream, ate the cresses that grew in bright pockets along its edge, and climbed to the peak to stare down over the coastal plains that housed Station One. I was too far away to see the actual Station but I knew where it was and, as I had countless times before, I imagined what life must be for my mother and brother or sister.

It took me three days to realise I had been a complete idiot not to take the Mech's weapon and that even without ammunition, it would have been a rare prize. The SciCorp survivors of the Fighting had been forced out of Station One with only the shirts on their backs and certainly without anything to reclaim their mothers, sisters and daughters, or the Station.

As well as the women and girls forced to stay at Station One some, like my mother, had chosen to stay. With my father dead and a baby on the way, she had good reason to remain in a place of safety. I did not begrudge her the choice she made but centuries ago, back on Earth, our ancestors' children were stolen by their conquerors and, no matter how much Lirra tried to soothe me, this second theft added to my fury.

Joseph reckoned the Mechs were happy to let us go because they expected us to die in the first winter. They could have killed the remaining SciCorp men and boys and forced their wives into a lifetime of rape but there was always a chance, no matter how remote, the Interstellar Judiciary ships would return.

Disputes on Sats were not uncommon, nor was mutiny, nor break-away groups setting up their own Stations, and while the Interstellar Judiciary often relocated the trouble-makers to less hospitable Sats in need of Settlers, they executed murderers.

The Fighting had been short but bloody. The Mechs had possession of the weapons store and the advantage of surprise and, unlike SciCorp, who were motivated by lofty ideals of planetary protection and the advancement of knowledge, the Mechs were motivated by arrash and coin.

They joined ships as Mech-crew to travel to far-flung Sats and do the hard work of establishing and maintaining the Stations, but they were always on the look-out for black-trade and inevitably had connections with the Trads, the big trader ships that operated outside Earth Space Corp, that arrived at night and were gone by morning.

When Earth had first claimed Compatible Planetary Systems, they had drawn up Declarations and Conventions and Accords to govern the use and protection of flora and fauna, the rights of sentient life-forms, and the maintenance of planetary integrity where Designated Essential Materials or DEMs were identified.

In the early days, Earth had the weaponry to enforce their edicts but as time went on, the steel-grey bulk of the Interstellar Judiciary ships filled Imago's skies less and less often until they disappeared altogether.

The Trads kept coming though, especially when the Mechs discovered what SciCorp had known all along: that Imago had arrash. According to Joseph, it was only pilfered at first, but the theft proved so profitable the Mechs began to plunder the Protection Zones. No one remembers whether SciCorp confronted the Mechs and that started the Fighting, or whether enough Mechs sucked up enough arrash to decide it would be a mighty fine idea to smash down everything they had built up.

No one remembers how long the Fighting lasted either or exactly how many were killed, not even Joseph, who labours over his recordings of our doings on Imago in charcoal ink on rast-bark paper.

Given that none of it matters any more, I reckon his scratchings simply help him pretend the nightmare that turned him from Station One's Chief Registrar into a cho-melon collector never really happened.

Whatever the numbers of dead from the Fighting, half a dozen boys like me, children of eleven or twelve, were effectively orphaned when our SciCorp fathers were killed and we were dragged from our mothers and thrown out of the Station. The Mechs kept the girl children to ensure the next generation of Mechs, all except one, and that girl child was Lirra.

And so, as summer gave way to winter, a shell-shocked group of scientists, biologists, geologists, botanists, mathematicians, physicists, chemists, astronomers, medicos and engineers; their wives, and a motley group of children, trudged away from the safe familiarity of Station One into the wild valleys and gorges of the Iron Ranges.

Joseph's a lot more precise when it comes to the actual numbers who made the trek and who went on to build Haven. Eighty-two in total, made up of forty men, twenty-three women and nineteen children, six of whom were without any parents at all.

Five years later we had grown to a hundred and four. Not a single life has been lost and of the twenty-two children born during this time, twenty had been girls. Joseph has this bizarre idea Imago has righted the sex balance because it wanted life to go on as before, but if that were true, the Sat would have thrown up a rock or striate branch to block the blast that killed my father. Anyway, we do not know how many children the Mechs have and given their easy lifestyle, it could be twice our number.

I would not have risked coin betting on our chances of survival after we were expelled but we were led by Micah Aristein, a mathematician and Jew whose ancestors, according to Joseph, had survived being hounded on Earth for hundreds of years.

Micah's mathematical expertise made him good at calculating the odds of any situation, but it took more than betting skills to keep despair at bay during those first desperate days. It took compassion, an air of quiet confidence, and a plan, and Micah had all three.

We had put two days of a hard, scrambling climb between us and Station One before Micah brought us to a halt on a small plateau on the ridge we later named Sanctuary Spur. The sun was setting as he gathered us about him and delivered his first real address since we had set out. His words were simple but have stuck in my head.

We are SciCorp, he said, and know where the wells are for water; where the cresses and lichens are that will feed us and heal our ills; where the tunnels are that will shelter us until our own pods are built; where the oil runs are for fuel and the matra for knives; where the rast grows that we must have for rope and clothes and covers.

In the years of Station One's existence, SciCorp has held true to our purpose of understanding and protecting all forms of life that are part of Imago, he ended solemnly, and this understanding, will now protect our own.

Or as Joseph later put it: 'The Mechs had brute force on their side but once the fighting was finished, that advantage no longer stood. A weapon was useless to a man who could not find water or food and we could find both.'

Joseph's words were probably true, but the reality was that while the Mechs had Station One, they had no need to search for anything, including water and food. Once established, Stations were designed to be more or less self-sustaining and at the time of the Fighting, Station One was pretty much ticking over by itself.

In fact, according to Joseph, Station One worked better than most Stations on other Sats, and he should know. As Chief Registrar, he had formulated reports on the Station's operations and sent them back to some mega repository on Earth and, before things had gone quiet, he had ensured that Station One met best practice.

But there was one duty he could not perform and the failure galled him. He could not add to the repository of data he was required to store on Imago because Imago had no Data Pod.

It had been sent separately by a contractor in accordance with Space Corp's standard protocols and not only contained a potted history of Earth's accomplishments in Commerce, Sciences, and the Arts, but data on Imago drawn from a multitude of sources. The trouble was the Data Pod had been lost soon after entry into Imago's atmosphere.

Joseph had searched as much of the Protection Zone as he could and begged the Station Commander to reconnoitre the further valleys. She had complied in the Station's early years but as time went on, she filed the pod as lost. In normal times Earth would have sent a replacement, but Earth's silence confirmed these were not normal times and no new pod ever arrived.

Joseph never gave up talking about it though or hoping the original pod would turn up and after Station One's records were lost to him as well, his quest for the Data Pod became an obsession.

A Gathering Pod was the first pod Micah got us to build at Haven. It had cooking fires at one end and facilities for sleeping, washing and waste disposal at the other. Looking back, I can see it was the simplest structure for us to put together.

There was enough fallen rast on the ridges to make saws unnecessary; enough ash slate in the valley pits to use as shingles; and enough rast bark from living trees to twist into ropes to hold the whole lot together.

Gaps in the walls were plugged with mud, a job assigned to SciCorp's children. I joined forces with Lirra, despite the catcalls of the other boys. Lirra's mother had chosen to remain at Station One too and our fathers' bodies had burned together in a massive pyre. But unlike me and the other boys, Lirra had escaped from Station One rather than been expelled.

She had chopped off her long hair and slipped in amongst us dressed in clothing stolen from a corpse. Being the only female child at Haven made her special but out-witting the Mechs made her a hero, something I could never be.

We chatted as we worked and never gave a thought to what would happen when the end of summer gave way to the start of winter; to how we would keep warm without our fibre-form jackets and boots; to how we would sleep without our temp-controlled beds.

Imago's mud was grey like much else on the Sat and we mixed it with rast fibres to bind it. They were too stiff for the job and despite our efforts, sprang back to spatter us with gloop.

'You are a muddy IFNO,' she laughed, after I copped another spray.

'A muddy IFNO is a MIFNO', I said, and added a few muddy lines across my cheeks as my ancestors had with ochre. She did the same.

'We are both MIFNO's now,' she said.

Earth's main export seemed to be acronyms and Station One ran on them. An IFNO was an Indigenous First Nations Oceania which meant that in Ancient times, Lirra and my ancestors had occupied a land in Oceania that had been over-run by non-indigenous peoples from Europa.

My parents' IFNO status had helped them meet a quota and get on a Settler Program and then on a ship, and there were quotas for virtually everything else including sexual identification, gender, age, marital status, colour, and religion. In contrast, skill quotas were dependent on the Designated Essential Materials or DEMs each new Sat was likely to contain, and making that particular judgement, was not very scientific at all.

By the time my parents joined the Settler Program, Earth had ceased its costly practice of sending Explorer Ships to carry out reconnaissance and sampling of newly discovered Sats. Instead, once a Sat had been identified as able to support human life without radical interventions such as atmospheric augmentation or ongoing nutriment supply, a general survey was undertaken by whatever ship was closest.

It might even be a Trad, happy to pick up the extra coin. Surveying Sats also gave the Trads the advantage of first plunder and a list of future black-trade ports.

Earth classified Sats as Botanic, Minralic or Mixed and Settler Ships delivered skill types accordingly. Settlers sent to Bot-Sats were mainly botanists, biologists, pharmacists and medicos whereas those sent to Min-Sats were dominated by geologists, chemists and metallurgists. Min-Sats' DEMs kept the great Earth ships plying their trade through space but Bot-Sats offered potential cures for a host of Earth's illnesses. According to Petar—one of Haven's medicos—Earth's illnesses multiplied faster than the secrets on Bot-Sat's could be unlocked.

Imago was classified as a Mix-Sat and as a botanist and a chemist, my parents were a good fit. Their IFNO status also meant the Space Settler Program could boast about being inclusive and, while that seemed to be important at the time, it was Imago's Mix-Sat status that was to prove crucial to the SciCorp exiles.

It meant we had a broad enough skill base to survive outside Station One. Geologists and chemists turned the oil runs into cooking and heating fires, botanists identified food sources, and pharmacists and medicos cured us of any sickness. And we had Joseph to write it all down for future reference.

The Gathering Pod remained a place of communal cooking and eating but as Haven grew, the washrooms and latrines were housed separately, and more pods were added to store food, house the equipment we laboriously constructed, host meetings, keep records and care for the sick. There were also pods for families and couples of whatever sexual orientation and larger pods for group housing for those of us who remained unpartnered.

I slept with the men, both old and young in one of these as I had since the early days of Haven, and Lirra slept with the women in another.

She had once raised the possibility of us moving to a couples' pod but when my lack of interest became plain, had not spoken of it again. I was seventeen then and my head so full of the injustices of the past that they left no room for the future.

The weather stayed fine up at the gorge, so I had no need of the crude shelter I had constructed. I spent most of my time on the sunny shelf of land staring down towards Station One, and the sprites grew so used to me they ceased their whistle calls of alarm and ignored me as they searched the bushes for leaf-eaters.

The scabs on my cheeks came off after four days but no matter how often I dunked my head in the stream's cool water, the welts remained, and by the end of the fifth day, I had to accept they were not going away.

It could have been the filth the Mech carried under his nails or that I had delayed too long in washing the wounds or some other reason. Lirra might know, for she was training as a medico, but I could hardly ask her. We had never lied to each other and I was not about to start now, but I did not want to tell her what I had done.

My tension grew as the daylight waned and my nerves were not helped by the sprites starting up their whistling again. My eyrie was open enough to prevent something creeping up on me, but the sprites' alarm calls did not quieten until the stars blossomed into a magnificent silvery vista.

The show was brief for the moons were waxing and their light soon robbed the stars of theirs. The smaller moon Diana rose first and then the monstrous glowing face of Hecate lurched into the sky, dwarfing Diana as usual. Their names came from some collection of Ancient gods, Joseph said, but no one knew why they had been chosen for Imago's moons. The information was probably in the lost Data Pod along with everything else it would have been handy to know.

I continued to scan my surroundings and caught the flash of something on the clefted peak above. My nerves were so taut I had dropped into a crouch before I realised it was only an argent-owl.

'Frightened of an owl, are you, Warrain?' I muttered, feeling foolish.

Imago's land mass, ocean and atmosphere were so similar to Earth's that it followed some of its creatures had evolved similarly, albeit with quirky differences.

Argent-owls shone like metal even when there were no moons and so tricked the dry-rats into thinking it was Hecate that hovered above them rather than a very efficient predator. At least that was what Sergei reckoned and he was a biologist, so he ought to know.

The owl took flight and the hair on the back of my neck shifted. I did not think I had startled it and the darkness suddenly seemed very thick. I could not see or hear anything but I gave up on the idea of sleep and sat propped against the stones for the rest of the night then started my journey back at first light.

It took me over a day to reach Haven because I went overland through the Striate Forests rather than back through the tunnels. Travelling through striate was like journeying through a forest of stone. No saplings sprouted through the detritus, no buds formed on the branches, no rotten trunks crashed to the forest floor. In all the time of Station One's existence, the trees had not changed at all.

Sergei insisted they had changed but they functioned at a rate too slow for us to measure, at least on Station One's instruments, and the trees did look alive with sprites nesting in them and insects hiding in their ridged bark.

Sergei said the maggots sheltered in them too after the Mechs had driven them from the coast, although I had never seen any. At least the trees themselves were in no danger from the Mechs: the wood turned out to be impossible to cut, impossible to burn, and almost impossible to access—thanks to the tunnel-riddled detritus.

In the early days of Station One, when SciCorp had worked out the taint in the river water came from the trees, the Mechs had been keen to blast them out of the valleys but the discovery of an aquifer near Station One had stopped them, as had SciCorp's prohibitions.

The Mechs could have gone ahead with their fireworks display after they expelled us and that they did not, raised hopes they had developed a more conservationist mentality. It was a theory that Dmitri, a chemist, scoffed at. If arrash was like other alpha opioids, he said, it would have a soporific effect over time. In other words, the Mechs were probably staggering about with eyes as cloudy as mudfish.

The Mech I killed certainly had not been dull and I had the marks on my face to prove it. I ran my fingers over my ridged cheeks as I walked and wished again I could come up with a believable story to explain them.

Travel through the striate might not have been easy but I had had plenty of practice navigating the detritus on other expeditions and the tangle meant I was unlikely to be seen by others except maggots perhaps.

Joseph took a keen interest in the maggots, probably because they gave him something else to write about, and anyone who spent time with Joseph knew all about them too, whether they wanted to or not.

I knew, for instance, that the arrival of the Explorer Ships had decimated their numbers because while Settler Ships had strict protocols governing First Contact with indigenous life forms, Explorer Ships had none at all, and they were always first to a new Sat.

The other problem for indigenous life forms was the galaxy remained a hazardous workplace and the Explorer Ships' crews were not inclined to risk their necks for small amounts of coin.

Their pay was double that of other ships and triple or even quadruple if the Commander was an Independent Affiliate of Space Corp. Running a fleet of Explorer Ships was expensive too, especially if years went by between finding DEMs, so Space Corp largely outsourced the explorer business to Independent Affiliates.

They sold the idea to concerned Earth citizens by insisting that Independent Affiliates operated within the strictest of protocols.

'A law unto themselves,' Joseph had said more than once.

As I grew older, it seemed to me the Settlers were not much better. During our voyage, we underwent only limited briefings on Imago's flora and fauna but extensive ones on how the Station was to operate.

It was clear in retrospect that the Settler Program was more about extracting Designated Essential Materials than protecting planetary integrity and advancing the knowledge of humankind, or whatever other platitudes Space Corp had dished up.

Joseph used the two-year voyage to access every holo on Imago's fauna and flora he could lay his hands on and had discovered the maggots had been a lot more maggot-like when the Explorer Ships had first arrived than when they had left.

Joseph's explanation for this was crude but probably accurate. Explorer Ships were crewed by men who might spend years in space between landings and so, when they found a Sat with a creature with roughly suitable anatomical structures, they had sex with it. In short, the Explorer Ship had arrived on a planet full of maggots and left a planet full of human-maggot hybrids.

'Just another Space Corp catastrophe to add to their craddy list,' he had muttered, for hybrids were sterile and that meant the maggots were doomed.

I had lived to be seventeen without setting eyes on one and there were few people in Haven who could claim any different. The Mechs had obviously come across them because they had plundered the maggots' arrash but the way Joseph spoke, you would think he was fully acquainted with them.

According to him, they grew as tall as an average human, had six appendages, two of which functioned like arms and four like legs, and had human-like faces.

But even with Joseph's description, I was completely unprepared for the sight of one, that day, in the Striate Forests.

etritus was not easy to travel over but it was not impossible either. You steered clear of rusty patches that indicated fal-lichen and shafts and aimed for the brownish-black areas that suggested a thickish roof over any subterranean tunnel.

No strategy was foolproof though and I had had a sleepless night. Add to that my worry over how to explain my injuries to Lirra and to any Mechs that might come looking for their missing comrade, and it was not a good combination.

I had reached a small slope without really noticing and it turned out to be unusually slick. I lost my footing, slid, grabbed at a striate and missed, and picked up enough speed to become airborne.

My flight was brief but when I hit the detritus again, it gave way, as I feared it would. Terror sealed my throat as I had visions of ending up with the Mech, but I only broke through one tunnel, and given the hardness of my landing, I guessed there were no more tunnels underneath. I did not notice my bruises until later though because I was not alone.

A maggot stood frozen just a few lengths from me, as shocked as I was by my sudden intrusion, and the hole I had smashed in the roof let in enough light for me see her clearly.

Her skin sheened with lustrous silver fur, very short and smooth, and her appendages were as human as mine, but ended in slender, dark coloured tips, not in hands and feet. At the time, I thought her torso was wrapped in a fine silver cloak, like the thermo blankets on the Settler Ship, but I found out later these were webs of hairless skin.

But it was her face that held me: silver faceted eyes, large and slanted with darker rims, nostrils but with no real nose, and a small human-shaped, lipless mouth. Stripes of dark fur ran from above each eye, broadening as they disappeared over her skull, and as she fled, I saw the pigmentation extended in two lines down her back.

The last glimpse of her also revealed a small, heart-shaped bulge at the base of her spine: the arrash pouch.

It was dusk when I finally reached Haven and despite being tired, I did not approach. Instead I circled around and reconnoitred from the tors higher up the slope. Nothing seemed amiss. People were finishing-up their work in the gardens and the red smoke that drifted from the Records Pod told me Joseph was in his usual place, hunched over his piles of rast bark.

Reassured, I made my way down and through the barrier of orshron leaves, careful to breathe through my mouth. Shadcats hated the smell of orshron and scattering leaves around Haven's boundaries was sufficient to keep them at bay. The smell was revolting to SciCorp too but you got used to it after a while and it beat being torn apart.

In the early days of Station One there had been dozens of attacks by shadcats or shadow cats as they were more properly called and they were the main reason for Station One's voltaged fence.

My father used to say they looked more like hyenas than cats but as I had never seen a cat or a hyena, not even on a holo, the comparison was useless. All I knew was shadcats were half as big as a man and had heavy front quarters, a sloping back, gingery fur, leathery skin and a poisonous bite.

Movement attracted them so if you were caught out in the open, your best defence was to freeze, if you could hold your nerve.

I headed across the yard towards the men's pod but at that moment, Lirra happened to come out of the Infirmary with Adrian. She had been working with Haven's medicos for close to a year and Adrian for almost two and they were deep in conversation. They probably discussed some medicinal lichen or other but I bristled. Adrian was twenty with all the easy- going confidence that came with being older and with being blessed with one of Haven's best smiles.

They stopped and there was a brief silence while two sets of medically-trained eyes fixed on my ridged cheeks, and then Adrian said something about catching up with Petar, nodded to me, and moved off.

'You chose a bad time to go walk about, Warrain,' said Lirra softly, her gaze still on my cheeks. 'We have had a visit from the Mechs.'

My throat was suddenly almost too tight it to speak. 'What did they want?' I managed to say.

'No one knows. They met with Micah and then left. Micah's made no announcements but he has pulled in Joseph, Mickey and Petar.'

I stared at her blankly. If the Mechs had threatened retribution, why would Micah confer with a record keeper, an astronomer, and a medico? He would be better advised to talk tactics with older men like Ewan who at least knew how to fight.

Lirra's brows drew in a frown. 'What have you done to your face?'

There it was; the question I had been dreading.

She ran her fingertips over the ridges. 'You have not put yourself through some sort of initiation rite, have you?'

'Of course not,' I snapped. There were men amongst the Ancients who had achieved manhood by killing, but not my ancestors. To become a man in the way they had, I would need to learn the secret lore of men and go to their sacred places and, since the death of Lirra's father and mine, there was no one on Imago to help me even part of the way.

Lirra's honey-brown eyes invited answers but I turned and strode off across the yard. She was not easy to shrug off though, her long legs keeping pace with mine. 'Tell me, Warrain.'

Her hand fastened on my arm and I swung back to her. 'I am hardly in a position to initiate myself, am I, Lirra, and given the lack of male IFNO's on Imago, I will be a boy until I die.' I virtually shouted the last part and Lirra recoiled. I was not much better, as shocked as she was by my outburst.

My parents had spoken little of the ceremonies their ancestors practiced thousands of years before but Lirra's had more than made up for it. She knew her people were from a different moiety to mine and that bloodlines had mattered a great deal in those times, as had the rituals that marked a girl as a woman, and a boy as a man.

She had worked with Joseph to ensure none of this data was lost and had wanted me to work with him too, but I had more important things to do like plot revenge against the Mechs.

17

My father was dead but the Mechs had not just robbed me of the feel of his stubbly face against mine and of his hand, light on my shoulder; they had robbed me of the image of what it was to be a man.

Of course, if all I needed was a role model there was Micah, who was admirable in every respect, but he did not share the memories embedded in my cells that stretched like a string of stars deep into the dark reaches of space.

These memories went back through countless cycles of births and deaths to campfires in red earth and corroborees under star-patterned skies; to the making of the world in songs as sure and powerful as the slide of the Rainbow Serpent or the arc of a throwing stick that found fire in the heavens and sent it crashing back to Earth.

Lirra waited and I took a steadying breath. 'I saw a maggot,' I said.

Her eyes widened but her tone was sardonic. 'A maggot and a Mech visit on the same day. We really are becoming popular. Where was it?'

'In a tunnel not far from here,' I said my tension easing. Until that moment, I had not realised the power of distraction.

'Was it as slimy as people say?' she asked. I knew Lirra backed Joseph's view the original maggots, if they were actually maggot-like, bore little resemblance to the fly larvae of Earth or to what now existed on Imago.

'She was about my height, with a humanish face and short silvery fur all over her,' I said. 'And she had black markings on the top of her head that ran down her back.'

'She? According to Joseph they are all "its" until the mating season when they become either male or female or they did before we came along. If it looked like a female, it might be some sort of residual chemical change from before they became hybrid.'

'Or Joseph might be wrong,' I retorted, disliking the way maggots were reduced to 'its', not that Lirra intended any disrespect; she simply repeated what Joseph said. Calling them maggots was hardly complimentary either nor was grubs which was what the Explorer Ships called them before they departed to wreck some other part of the galaxy in the name of civilisation.

'You need to tell Joseph,' said Lirra. 'I do not think maggots have ever been sighted around here. She frowned, as she always did when she was thinking. 'There might even be more of them about unless it was the last one. Another triumph for Space Corps' Protection Zone policies,' she added bitterly, and then her eyes refocused on my cheeks. 'Where have you been?'

'In the Ranges,' I said.

'Did you argue with Hans again?'

Hans and I had never got on, even as children, and since he had decided to train as a scientist, he had taken every opportunity to explain to ignorant people like me how the planet actually functioned.

He knew about the minerals that fed the different lichens and the chemical composition of the oil runs, but he did not know how the lichens warned of shafts or how oil runs fed cake-flowers, which in turn fed ghost-bats whose roosts kept dry-rats and wrell-wasps at bay and so made good shelters for the likes of me. Hans was all about facts not feelings and he had never heard of self-doubt.

'Sometimes I need to be on my own,' I muttered. It had been the reason I set off down the tunnels but not the reason I had stayed away so long.

'And sometimes I need you with me,' she said softly.

My heart quickened but before I could think of a response, she shrugged and made off towards the gardens. Micah did not forbid anyone at Haven going deeper into the Ranges or into the valleys or tunnels for that matter, but someone had to cover their workload in their absence. No complaints were ever made but I would be working doubly hard over the next few weeks to pay back the time.

There was no point stewing over what the Mechs might have said to Micah, so I headed off to the composting pits. These were the least popular workplaces and labour was always needed to aerate the stinking mass of effluent, food scraps and harvest waste. Rosco was there as usual and for the first time I noticed how bent he was.

His hand where he gripped the hook-rake was criss-crossed with veins as tangled as the tunnels and he still wore a rast hat like those we fashioned before we learned better ways to soften and mould the fibres.

Rosco had been old even before the Fighting killed his friends and robbed him of any joy and as I grabbed a hook-rake and started to work, it struck me that I had never seen him smile. This day was no exception, although he did speak, which was unusual, though not until we were working together by moonlight.

'They want Haven,' he said.

I stopped my heaving of the putrid layers and leaned on the rake. 'Who wants Haven?' I asked, but I already knew he meant the Mechs. But after five long years, why steal Haven now? Even as the question banged about in my head, I knew the answer: because they could.

They had weapons and we did not, but they also had something far more lethal that we lacked: a willingness to kill. This failing had turned out to be a fatal flaw for SciCorp except I had somehow inherited the murder-gene.

My blood boiled like a fire-heated oil run at the prospect of being robbed of my home a second time and I silently pledged I would kill again and again, rather than let it happen.

'Micah would know the odds by now,' went on Rosco, as if he spoke to himself. 'He will keep us alive to start again somewhere else but we will lose the women this time. The Mechs have seen what we have got.'

My heart pounded so hard I had to steady myself against the rancid wall. It was a fury fed not just by the theft of my immediate family or of Station One's comforts, but by more ancient thefts committed thousands of years before on Earth.

'What does Micah say?' I managed to choke out, but Rosco had gone back to his work and silence. I felt like grabbing him by the throat like I had grabbed the Mech and shaking him until he confessed he had lied, that the Mechs had not visited, and we were safe to enjoy what five years of unremitting toil had carved out for us.

Instead, I thrust my hook-rake deep into the mix, digging and turning with all my strength until the sweat poured off me, and I continued to work long after Rosco had taken himself off to wash, and eat and sleep. Lamps burned in the Gathering Pod and I could hear the murmur of conversations as if nothing had changed, but the spill of light from the Meeting Pod told me Micah was still at his desk.

How bitter it must be for him as he worked his way methodically through his endless calculations: the odds of us defending Haven, the time it would take to build another Station, whether he had enough years left in him to accomplish it a second time. But there would be no point in starting over.

If they took the women, we would die off anyway, and why bother building something the Mechs could steal again and again whenever the mood took them.

I stopped to draw breath and feeling the effects of almost a week subsisting on cress, stowed the rake and went to the washroom to scrub myself clean. As I washed, I contemplated that I did not actually know why the Mechs had come, and their visit might not be a bad sign after all.

Maybe they wanted to reconcile with us and had offered some kind of olive branch in the way of the Ancients; maybe they needed our expert help and had come to trade something for it.

We had all the medical knowledge and held all the information about Imago's plants and animals and minerals and we had learned a lot more in the last five years. Station One had been designed by Mechtechnicians on Earth and much of it was automated but at Haven, we had been forced to live without such luxuries.

Earth had abandoned us long before the Mechs had thrown us out of Station One, but we no longer had any need of Earth or the Mechs, I told myself, because we understood Imago.Looking back I can see how breath-takingly arrogant I was. As if we did understand Imago, as if anyone or anything could understand Imago, except perhaps the striate. But I was desperate then as I stood in the washroom and considered everything I had to lose.

I wanted to trade fear for hope, to believe the Mechs had come to ask nicely for something we could offer them and to negotiate with us like honourable men, not murder us and steal it afterwards.

I made my way across the yard towards the Gathering Pod but stopped short of it, reluctant to enter despite my grumbling belly. The pod might hold news of what the Mechs had said to Micah whereas out here, I could still pretend nothing had changed.

The moons' gilded faces filled the sky, but I stared past them to where I imagined Earth must be. My father had held me aloft as a little boy and named the star systems and told me how we were at one end of the galaxy and how Earth was at the other, and I had imagined I could return home like I could walk from one end of Sapphire Bay to the other, if I pushed on, if I ignored the ache in my legs.

I was so taken up with the naiveté of my childish self, I did not notice Joseph come up beside me until he spoke. 'Everything has changed,' he said softly.

'The Mechs?' I said harshly, jerking round.

'Them too.'

He stared up at Imago's moons and his face was filled with such wonder I thought he had found the Data Pod. Then I followed his gaze and my breath caught. There was a third moon there, as gold as Hekate but many times smaller and just visible beyond Hekate's mighty glow.

'Everything has changed,' he repeated, and smiled.

5

Micah called the meeting the next morning in the Gathering Pod and everyone went, even the children. They were quiet and not just because they were in awe of Micah but because the meeting was brief. I stared at Micah as he made his way in, searching for signs of anger or resignation in his face, but he looked calm.

Micah was not a tall man, but he had never got his authority from bluff or bluster. Joseph said that, as a Jew, Micah carried the means of his survival embedded in his genes and it was this that made him a natural leader, but that made no sense to me.

If Jews had been persecuted on Earth they were hardly likely to be better loved elsewhere in the galaxy given humans carried their prejudices with them. I do not think Micah being a Jew was the reason for the respect he enjoyed at all.

The Settler Ships had quotas of religious and ethnic groups, genders, and sexual orientations, but once onboard, the divisions became largely irrelevant. Two years of being crammed together meant friendships and antagonisms were based on things other than Ancient stories of data-inscribed stones being handed down from the sky by equally Ancient gods.

People worshipped alone if they worshipped at all and, unless they carried their holy books with them, the records of their beliefs and practices had been lost with everything else in the Data Pod.

But I was not thinking about any of these things as Micah took his place at the far end of the Gathering Pod. I was waiting for him to raise his finger and point at me, and for those of Haven to turn and stare at the young man who, in having murdered, had brought the Mechs up from Station One to murder them in turn.

Micah looked at me but he also looked at everyone else in the pod, as was his custom. Whenever he spoke, whether it was to a group of children or to those too decrepit to raise their eyes, his gaze included all his audience.

'As you know, we have had a visit from Station One,' he said. 'The visit comprised three Mechtechnical Officers: Second Commander Nathan Cohen, Third Commander Tom Fernandez, and Leading Mechtech Seth McKenzie.' Micah paused, presumably to let the names and ranks of the Mechs sink in but to most of Haven they were simply thieves and murderers.

'There is sickness at Station One and they seek our aid.'

I was so relieved Micah's next words contained nothing about a missing Mech that it took a moment for their meaning to sink in. I heard Lirra hiss beside me but her face bore excitement rather than animosity.

She saw an opportunity to practice her medico skills and, I realised with a jolt, it made no difference to her whether she practiced them on us or on those who had stolen her family.

I started to remind her exactly what the filthy crads had done but was drowned out by the uproar which consisted of sentiments very similar to mine: it was fitting the Mechs died; it was probably arrash poisoning so let them rot; the Mechs' visit risked infecting us; going to Station One risked bringing the illness back to Haven; the Mechs could not make us help them and if we did help them, we should extract a heavy price.

Micah let the debate rage but I saw the glances he exchanged with Joseph, Petar and Mickey. As Haven's record keeper Joseph had the greatest breadth of knowledge about everything and Petar was a medico so it made sense for Micah to seek his advice too, but I had no idea why he involved Mickey who was an astronomer.

Micah waited for the hubbub to die down before he spoke again. 'I have had longer than you to consider our options,' he said, 'and as I see it, each carries particular risks. To refuse help is to invite those of Station One to take it anyway.

'All they need do is to use hostages to assure themselves of our cooperation or they could take our medicos and kill any who oppose them. Or, if they believe Station One to be contaminated, they could relocate to Haven and expel us, or let us remain but murder those of us they see as a threat.

'If we are expelled, we could rebuild, but there is nothing to prevent those of Station One dispossessing us again. While they have weapons and we do not, the possibility remains.'

There was silence while we digested this bitter fact. No one argued because anyone with any grip on reality had already reached the same conclusions.

'We could refuse to help and hope those of Station One die quickly, and that whatever afflicts them remains on the coast,' Micah's emotionless voice went on. 'We might even, in the fullness of time, be able to reclaim Station One, although we would need to be very sure it was not contaminated.

'Or we could offer aid in return for some sort of concession, such as them leaving us in peace. However, we are not in a strong bargaining position. Or we could offer aid because it is the right moral and ethical thing to do.

'This could build goodwill that might save us from future violence but, given our history together, there is no guarantee of that either.'

'You are assuming there is a cure for whatever afflicts them,' said Hans.

'Maybe it is arrash poisoning,' offered Adrian, and mutters of "serve them right" rose from the gathering.

'The long-term effects of arrash are unknown,' whispered Lirra, 'but if it is like other alpha opioids, it will not make them sick while they are using it or having treatment. Maybe they have run out.'

'What did you think of the Mechs that visited, Micah?' Judith's powerful voice rang out and silence fell as people perceived the importance of the question. If the Mechs had come swaggering in, our choices were more limited than if they had come with some semblance of respect.

Judith had been widowed by the Fighting but had been too old for child-bearing and the Mechs had let her go. I think she had been a biologist before but I had only ever known her as Haven's cook. Even seeing her away from the kitchens was odd.

'They seemed willing to be polite,' said Micah drily. 'My feeling is that at this stage, the Mechtechnical Officers simply want the illness that afflicts them resolved. They have had three deaths so far and four others are in their Infirmary.'

'What have they used to treat the sickness?' asked Lirra.

'SI 22.'

SI 22 meant nothing to me and I suspect it meant nothing to anyone in Haven without an excellent memory. The Settler Ships had Standard Issues or SI's of all sorts of things ranging from clothing to medicines, the latter with self-replicating capacities. Earth's medicos concocted seed-chemicals for dispatch to the far-flung corners of the galaxy, each batch designed to protect Settlers from a range of common threats, but nothing was foolproof.

In the early days of Sat settlement, the SI's were tailored to each Sat's particular requirements, but then Space Corp decided it would be cheaper to augment SI's with Settlers' ingenuity or luck, where their needs were unique. It was also cheaper to let Settlers die, especially if they died a long way away.

After we were expelled from Station One, our medicos had searched Imago's flora for cures to common ailments and I had spent a lot of time with Lirra roaming the Ranges, tunnels and Striate Forests helping them.

I had a good eye for things that were subtly different as had Lirra. She reckoned it was an IFNO trait and she was probably right; hunting and gathering having lingered longer in our ancestors than in their conquerors.

'The Mechtechnical Officers do not think the illness is contagious,' went on Micah. 'Their ill have come from different families in different parts of the Station.'

'And you believe them?' challenged Rosco. He spoke so rarely that people stared. 'Maybe they have left us a gift. Some slimy bug to finish us off.'

There were murmurings and an exchange of worried glances.

'All things are possible,' acknowledged Micah, 'but as they have left us in peace these last five years, I do not think it is likely. They seemed genuinely worried. There is the question of arrash, of course, and the danger those who are arrash-affected pose to any of Haven who offer aid.'

A new wave of muttering arose. There was an ongoing debate over whether the Mechs murder and expulsion of their fellow Settlers was a result of the opioid or of their inherently brutish natures, and the argument continued to divide Haven. I did not care. I simply hoped the Mechs continued to use arrash and it poisoned them.

SciCorp had been instructed to investigate Imago's version of the alpha opioid because it was classed as a Designated Essential Material—medical use, although my father believed it was only a DEM because it was prized as black-trade.

He also believed Space Corp had its fingers in the whole black-trade industry and was just as complicit as the Trad ships in the decimation of a Sat's resources. It explained how they slipped between the star systems and Space Corp's laws and protocols with equal ease.

I could not remember whether the Mechs who shouted and fired their weapons during the Fighting carried the odour that clings to arrash-users like a foul perfume, or whether they shouted in triumph at having rid the Station of those who controlled it and them.

Again, Micah waited patiently for the exchanges to die down. 'The Mechtechnical Officers who visited were not arrash-affected and suggested easily attainable supplies of arrash are exhausted. It also appears the Commander of Station One has no liking for it.'

I do not think this was good news to anyone for I was not alone in hoping the Mechs continued to abuse their health and the arrash would lead to their demise.

Station One ticked over with little human intervention and I had fondly imagined that, at some point, we would simply walk back in and reclaim everything we had lost.

'I will leave you to consider our options,' said Micah, 'and will be in the Admin Pod if you would like to discuss things further. The Mechtechnical Officers are to return the day after tomorrow and I have undertaken to give them our response then.'

People went about their tasks for the rest of the day but Haven had a subdued air about it and people could be seen whispering together in odd corners. I went back to the compost pits as did Rosco, but he had withdrawn into his usual silence and I was left to my own thoughts. I would have liked to talk to Lirra but she did not seek me out and I could not blame her. The compost pits were the least inviting places in all of Haven.

Since choosing to train as a medico, Lirra spent most of her time with Haven's established medicos, Petar and Thi. She was nineteen but even exiles of fifteen and sixteen had started to attach themselves to men or women with particular expertise, in unofficial apprenticeships.

And it was necessary. Haven did not have the benefit of Station One's systems. Everything we learned as exiles must be recorded, practised and passed on.

Joseph had tried in all sorts of subtle ways to arouse my interest in a range of roles and Adrian had ribbed me in all sorts of unsubtle ways about my lack of SciCorp attributes, but the more they pushed, the more I pushed back, either disappearing into the Ranges for days on end or picking up Haven's least skilled work.

I wonder now, looking back, whether I knew that training to be Haven's next this or that meant accepting I would never return to Station One. I also wonder whether I sat up in the Tors so often and watched the moons paint their milky paths across the water because I yearned for Earth. I had been too young when we left to have conscious memories of it but unconscious ones were encoded in my genes, not that Space Corp cared about such things.

They tick-boxed their pastoral care obligations to the Settlers by compiling records of the Settlers' familial, aesthetic and spiritual needs and sending these off on the Settler ships in the Data Pods. The loss of our Data Pod did not concern me as I had my parents to give me a sense of who I was and while they had both spoken of the place called Australia, where the red desert sands had imprinted my bloodline for thousands of years, it was my father's memories that proved the most potent.

'You are your father's son,' my mother used to say to me but it had taken Lirra to explain what that actually meant and then I saw my mother was right, and it was my father's memories that became my own.

How accurate they were in the first place I do not know. My parents' families had been urban for generations or else my parents would never have been selected as Settlers. Even so, at least once a year my father went back to his country, to sit in the red sand and to stare at stars that sang his Dreaming, and it was on one of these trips that he met my mother who, like him, was drawn back to her country time and time again.

I worked steadily with the hook-rake but as the day drew on, became increasingly frustrated at Lirra's non-appearance. I wanted to talk to her and, as my anger grew, I decided she obviously did not want to talk to me.

Despite Micah framing our situation as if we had choices, it was clear the Mechs could come with their weapons anytime they wanted and take Haven, or take our medicos and women, or take whatever else they chose exactly as they had done before.

The sun sank and as the sky took on its usual emerald and purple lustre, I went to the washroom, scrubbed myself down and strode away from Haven. Anything seemed preferable to waiting for the Mechs to exert their will, which might explain why I headed for the valley where I had seen the maggot, despite knowing my chances of seeing another one was close to zero.

The valleys had little to recommend them. They gave no views of Sapphire Bay and hemmed you in with endless rows of striate and craddy piles of detritus. It was almost dark by the time I reached the striate and I had to use lumin-lichen to guide my descent. Even so, I could not be sure the tunnel I found was the same one I exited and I stopped and strained for sound.

Imago's fauna ranged from stone-mice up to owls and shadcats and, while I had a healthy respect for shadcats, and admired the argent-owls' silvery swoops, it was Imago's flora that drew me. Not that

I let my interest in it be known. The last thing I wanted was Haven's biologists badgering me about following in their footsteps.

I started up the valley looking for other tunnel entrances, having to wedge myself sideways to fit through the striate; their massive boles and the lack of new trees making the gaps between them tight.

There must have been a time when the trees had been small, when there had been blossom and seed and new shoots uncurling; when roots had stretched down into Imago's grey earth. A time when the striate had taken from the soil what they needed to strike skyward towards Imago's sun and twin moons, but that time was not now, and with the arrival of the third moon, twin moons were about to join striate saplings in being completely out of fashion.

I stared up at the moons through chinks in the canopy as I went. Why would another moon appear anyway? Then again why not? The Data Pod probably had records of its orbit as well as the orbits of its sister moons.

It was just that we did not have the Data Pod. The craddy Data Pod again! I was starting to sound like Joseph. I took a steadying breath and ran my fingers across my ridged cheeks. Nothing much had happened on Imago since the Fighting and then Mechs had got sick and paid us a visit, a third moon had appeared, and I had seen my first maggot. And I had murdered.

'Kill or be killed,' I muttered, trying to still the churn of my guts. The Mech had reached for his weapon but even had he extended his hand in friendship I would not have extended mine. I had had no choice, I repeated. Only the Mechs had choice, only the craddy Mechs with their weapons!'

I dragged my seething thoughts back to the less threatening subject of the maggot. While they were the most advanced of Imago's sentient life forms, they certainly were not intelligent enough to outwit shadcats and for the first time I wondered why the shadcats did not attack them.

Maybe the maggots had some sort of chemical in their bodies shadcats had learned to avoid. Anders, one of SciCorp's biologists, had told me that on Earth, there had been a butterfly so toxic the birds' inherited memories warned subsequent generations to keep away. Perhaps it was the same with maggots and shadcats.

I wondered whether the original maggots had the same defence mechanism or whether only the hybrids did, assuming the current crop of maggots were hybrids. SciCorp had never been able to test the theory either.

Protocols prohibited the tranquilizing, trapping or confinement of sentient life forms that had already been classified, and maggot sightings had grown rare after the Mechs plundered the Protection Zone.

Something moved to my left and I froze. For a horrible moment, I thought it was a Mech, and their tale of sickness had simply been a ruse to draw me away from Haven's protection and finish me off.

I searched frantically for a non-existent striate branch to use as a weapon then realised it was no Mech that stood in the shadows but a maggot, in fact, the maggot. I stared at her and she stared back at me.

She did not seem frightened this time and I wondered whether she was sick. There was illness at Station One and I now faced a maggot that did not flee, seemed too much of a coincidence.

I took a step forward, wanting to end the strange hiatus, but the maggot stood her ground and as the moons' rose higher, their light showed no signs of sickness in the maggot's lustrous fur.

And then her small lipless mouth moved. 'Warrain.'

I gaped at her. My brain insisted she had not said my name, but my ears disagreed. The sound was sibilant, not slurred exactly, but smudged over, as if distorted by wind through the striate, except there was no wind.

Maggots were dumb, could not speak, would not know my name, would not linger, would not try to communicate. I watched her mouth open again, watched it frame a sound that could only be my name.

'Warrain! Where the crad are you?' It was Lirra and in the split second I looked away, the maggot was gone. 'Warrain!'

I heard the rattle of pebbles as Lirra made her descent and then the crunch of detritus as she reached the edge of the striate. I did not answer, my head too full of the maggot's voice.

Lirra emerged from the shadows above me and I managed to jerk my brain into gear.

'Warrain?' Her voice was filled with concern now as she came the last of the way down.

'Are you all right?'

'Yes.'

'Why are you here?'

'For all the usual reasons.'

'Which are?'

'You know me, Lirra,' I said with a shrug. 'I am looking for answers where there are none, for a way back when the way is closed, for some escape from dying here.' For something that was stolen from my bloodline thousands of years ago, and again five years ago, and probably will be again in the coming days.

'We will both die here, Warrain. It is our home.'

'It will never be mine.'

'Not if you do not allow it,' she said gently. She was close enough now for her breath to warm my cheek and I turned my face away. I heard her sigh, quick and impatient, and the crack of detritus as she stepped back. 'I have decided to go,' she said abruptly. 'I will tell Micah tomorrow.'

'Go?'

'To Station One, to sort out what is happening there.'

'You cannot—' I began.

'I can, and I will. It is logical and it is what Micah wants. We cannot afford to risk experienced medicos like Petar or Thi. If the Mechs are playing some sort of game, they might kill them or prevent their return.

'I am willing to bet my skills are greater than any the Mechs have and they are not likely to kill good breeding stock like me. And if the Mechs are after Haven, it will give me a chance to find out. It will buy us time, Warrain.'

'This is idiocy,' I exclaimed. 'You are not to go!'

'Idiocy, is it?' Her voice held an edge I had not heard before. 'It is better than hiding in the Striate Forests.'

'I am not hiding!'

'Yes, you are. It is all you have ever done. Hidden from what you are, from what we both are!'

'I have never been ashamed of being IFNO,' I said furiously.

'I am not talking about that,' she said impatiently. 'I am talking about Imago. Your parents and mine made a decision to join a Settler Ship, to use their skills on a Sat that needed protection.

'They kept faith with those ideals and it cost them dearly. It is irrelevant they were IFNO's. It is irrelevant we are IFNO's. No one cares that Micah's a Jew, that Thi is a Buddhist, that Joseph is a Christian. They kept the faith, they still keep the faith and the faith is to care for Imago!'

She took a steadying breath. 'They got on a Settler Ship and came here. Even if Earth had not gone quiet, they would not have gone back, they could not. It was part of the contracts they signed. For better or worse, they committed to Imago, and they committed us along with them. This is our home ,Warrain and we owe it our protection.'

Lirra's eyes shone as brightly as the maggot's although I did not see the similarity at the time; the dangers of her naive idealism had wiped the maggot from my mind. Micah would not let her go, I comforted myself. He was not a fool.

I said nothing and muttering something about leaving me to sulk alone, Lirra stomped back up through the striate.The night was old before I returned to Haven and as I crawled into bed, I wished for the first time I had taken up Lirra's suggestion and asked Micah for a couples' pod. There was a lot of talk amongst the men and the last thing I wanted to hear was even more stuff about what the craddy Mechs were likely up to, what Micah could do in response, and what the outcomes might be, none of which were optimistic.

It took me a long time to get to sleep and when I woke, the pod was mostly deserted. I was tempted to stay in bed, but the previous night's events crowded in on me and I got up and went to the Gathering Pod to breakfast.

The talk there was much the same but the women were quieter, swallowing their fears rather than speaking them aloud. They glanced at Micah often though, their faces full of anxiety.

Lirra sat apart with Petar and Thi and it did nothing to improve my temper when Adrian joined them. I glowered into my zitin and only looked up when Joseph's bowl clanged down on the table next to mine.

'Decision day,' he announced, and when I glanced at him sourly, added: 'You saw how big it was last night?' For a moment, I thought he was talking about the maggot, then I realised he referred to the third moon. 'If we had access to the 'scopes at Station One, we would be able to tell a lot more about it.'

'Such as?'

'Whether it is related to the present two and if not, where it has come from. It might even tell us the origins of Imago's existing moons. In any case, Micah will need to decide who is to map its movements.'

'Micah's got more important things to do than worry about stray moons.'

'No moon is stray,' corrected Joseph. 'They all belong somewhere. And I am wondering if it is alone or whether there are others following it.'

I stopped eating. 'Why would there be others?'

'For the same reason as Imago has Diana and Hekate, and Earth the Moon. They might be chunks that broke off during the bangs of planetary birth or have been flung off some other event in deep space and been hurtling along on their own until they came within Imago's pull.

'Our moons have similar orbits despite Hekate being many times bigger than Diana and that means their compositions must be different, and that means they probably have different origins. This new moon might come from the same place as one of Imago's existing moons, or from somewhere else.

'It might pass us by or Imago might capture it. And depending on its mass, it might pull Imago out of its solar orbit.'

I was only half listening to Joseph's meandering commentary, but this last fact jolted me. 'And if it did?' I asked.

'Everything would change. At the moment, we have a day-length similar to Earth's and seasonal changes like Earth's mid latitudes but even a small deviation would alter all that. A new moon is always an interesting thing to throw into the mix,' he ended cheerfully.

'Is there any way of working out how close the new moon will pass?'

'Not with any certainty. Micah can work wonders with his bead machine but even it might not be up to the task. But the Mechs could if they had the skill and the inclination.

'There are enough data computes in Station One to make the calculations, but I doubt the Mechs have even noticed we have a visitor. They were never very interested in star-gazing and the new moon is pretty much still obscured by Hekate.'

I had never taken much interest in Imago's planetary system either, nor had I need to, not when I was surrounded by members of SciCorp who lived and breathed the stars and who spent weeks poring over data-slabs at Station One and, when they were lost to them, over data generated by cruder instruments.

'Do you think the Mechs want Haven?' I blurted out.

'The Mechs have got everything they need at Station One,' he said, 'and a pleasant backyard to play in. Nice flat land, fresh water, and the sea. The Ranges are not nearly as attractive to them.'

'Except they have not got sickness.'

I watched Joseph closely, scarcely aware of how much I yearned for the reassurance that no one in their right mind would give up Sapphire Bay for the striate and detritus-filled valleys of the Ranges, but the reassurance did not come.

'What you say is true,' he said. 'If the Mechs believe the sickness is linked to Station One, they will want to be free of it and, even if they do not want to leave Station One, now they have seen Haven, they might fancy it for themselves. Or they might simply flex their muscles and expel us just because they can.'

I shoved my bowl of zitin away. 'And we are going to let them?'

'They have weapons.'

'And we have matra knives and the high ground. We could ambush them, get in first for once. They would not be expecting it especially if they have sickness.'

'Micah would never agree to that,' he said.

'No,' I said bitterly. 'He would just walk away without a whimper and make us start all over again.'

'Micah kept us alive last time and he will do whatever is necessary to keep us alive this time, if it comes to that.'

'Is that all you want?' I demanded. 'Just to stay alive? To work until your hands bleed to make a place for yourself and have it stolen from you over and over again?'

'Staying alive is no bad thing,' said Joseph dourly, and pushed his seat back. 'Let us hope you get to grow old enough to realise that.'

I glowered at Joseph's retreating back. The pod was full of people like him, already calculating how many of their possessions they could carry away in their packs.

I returned to the compost pits to work but my nerves were on edge. The Mechs were due back tomorrow and before then, Micah had to decide what we would do.

I got stuck into the mess with my hook-rake, but my heart was not in it. For once Rosco was absent and I guessed he was in the men's pod sorting through the things he had managed to accumulate in his time in Haven. There would not be much.

Micah did not call the meeting until that evening and by then Haven was awash with rumours. We were all to leave that night; stay put and refuse aid; send someone to assess the illness or Micah was to go to Station One himself and report back, and so on.

Lirra's threat to take herself off to Station One niggled at me but I had dismissed the idea as ridiculous by the time I scrubbed off the stench of the compost pits and sat down to eat.

Lirra was not there but she often ate at midmeal and spent the evenings going over the records Joseph created. Even so, my skin prickled. People were clearly nervous and I wondered, as they probably did, whether this would be our last meal together in the pod we had built, off the platters we had fired, in the community we had laboured so hard to establish.

The tables were being cleared before Micah rose from his seat and the pod hushed in an instant. 'A proposition has been put to me I have reluctantly accepted,' he said, without preamble, as was his habit. 'I hope it resolves the dual threats the sickness at Station One presents, firstly, that we too will become ill and secondly, those of Station One will seek to take Haven.

'I am aware of what might unfold but I believe we should at least seek to resolve the issue of Station One's illness first, rather than react to something that might never eventuate.'

He paused to let his words sink in, and it seemed to me that no one in the pod breathed. 'As you know, Haven has the benefit of two highly experienced medicos, Petar Ivanko and Thi Nguyen, and two medicos in training, Adrian Adamson and Lirra Gnattarre.

'Adrian and Lirra have volunteered to accompany the Mechtechnical Officers back to Station One to investigate the nature of the sickness there. While Adrian and Lirra are still in training, they are sufficiently skilled to offer immediate aid and, if necessary, accurately report their findings to Petar and Thi who will then offer further assistance.'

'No!' The word was out of my mouth before I could stop it. People stared but something had ignited in my guts and the fire grew with every second. 'You cannot let Lirra go. It is not safe!'

'She is not going alone, Warrain,' said Micah, in his usual unruffled tone.

'You cannot let her go!' I repeated, knowing I sounded like a petulant child.

'Nor can I prevent her,' said Micah. 'We at Haven are free to come and go as we wish. Lirra is determined to go and she will have Adrian with her.'

'Adrian? What use will he be?'

A mutter ran through the pod, but Micah continued to regard me calmly. 'He will be as much use as any of us. None of us are armed, Warrain, but I do not believe the Mechtechnical Officers mean us harm, at least not yet.

'They seem concerned only with curing those who are ill. We have had no contact with them for five years, no visits to wish us well, no attacks to finish us off, no attempts to drive us further away. Our best chance of retaining what we have, Warrain, is to help those of Station One.'

His words were true but the fire in my guts had spread and even drawing breath was difficult. Having finished his meal and his announcement, Micah made his way out of the pod and others followed him, but I stayed where I was, my chest heaving as if I had run. I knew I was making a spectacle of myself and even Joseph avoided looking at me as he exited the pod.

I wanted to find Lirra and demand she remain, but she was probably with Adrian, planning what they would do when they reached Station One or planning their life together. My hands balled into fists but even as the blood roared in my ears, I realised the closeness Lirra and I had shared since childhood had fractured well before Adrian came on the scene.

I prowled around the empty pod and the painful truth hit me that the cracks in our friendship had started back when Lirra had chosen to become a medico. And it was not just that she started to spend more time with Petar and Thi and Adrian, but that she had found a sense of purpose I lacked. Her new-found maturity sat as easily around her shoulders as a possum-skin cloak, while my shoulders remained bare.

I stared sightlessly at the pod. No lamps had been lit for there was no need, not with the double dose of moonlight that streamed in through the windows. It filled the room with a coldness that seemed to hint at a desolation to come.

I strode out of the pod, slamming the door behind me, and headed for the Tors. My shadow ran before me, cast dark by the moons' brilliance. Hekate was huge and Diana jostled at her shoulder and while the third moon had grown, it was still hard to see unless you knew where to look.

The way was steep, but it did not take me long to reach the spot where the shards of exposed stone speared skyward. The Tors had been a favourite haunt of the boys who had marched away from Station One five years ago and of Lirra, and I still came here to take advantage of the view over Sapphire Bay.

The ocean was afire with moonlight and I could even see the twinkle of Station One's lights. Not lamps illuminated by ampha seed but by lith cells that would last as long as the planet.

I had gazed down over the coast countless times before but tonight I sensed something had changed and, as I looked beyond Sapphire Bay to Amethyst and Turquoise Bays, the feeling strengthened.

Maybe it was the horror of knowing that Lirra, whose bravery as a child had allowed her to escape the Mechs, was to put herself back under their stinking control and that Micah, whose job it was to protect her, had agreed. And it was okay with him, apparently, because Adrian was to go with her!

Adrian! A man who had never explored the tunnels like I had, who had never seen a maggot, who did not know the subtle variations in lichens that I knew or their effects; a man whose knowledge came from what Joseph said, not from laying his hands on the soft stems of cress or on the wiry ones of lichen, not by feeling the heart of things.

The night was old before I returned to Haven. I took a circuitous route back and detoured again when I got there, visiting the food stores in the Gathering Pod before going to my bed and sleeping a heavy, dreamless sleep.

It was still early when I woke and in contrast to my anger and confusion of the previous night, I knew exactly what I was going to do. I dressed, took a pack from the store, and filled it with a spare set of clothes, a canteen of water and several pouches of zitin. I was tempted to slide my matra blade into my boot, but I did not want to lose it. A matra blade was useless against weapons anyway.

If I had been going to confide my intentions to anyone it would have been Joseph, but I was in no mood for argument or being thwarted. Instead, I found an empty table near the back of the Gathering Pod and started on my breakfast. My vantage point gave me a good view of Lirra and Adrian as they ate with Micah and ensured the other diners hid me from their view.

The slight knit to Lirra's brows told me she concentrated on whatever Micah was saying and I noticed she had cut her hair. She wore it short anyway but the cut gave her tighter curls that accentuated her full lips and the graceful sweep of her neck.

Adrian looked pale in comparison and soon excused himself and disappeared out the door. I continued to watch Lirra and my attention settled on her hands. She had slender hands that usually flapped about her like ghost-bats but now lay quiet on the table, their stillness like the last moments of calm before a storm.

Most of Haven's inhabitants were breakfasting when Ewan escorted the Mechs in. Silence fell and while the conversations slowly picked up, the tension in the room was palpable.

I assumed the Mechs were the same three who had visited previously and while Micah had been meticulously polite in giving them their correct titles, to me they would simply become Boss Cohen, Deputy Fernandez and Underling Seth.

All three were muscular and wore Station One's form-fitting fibre-suits, and they were armed. Cohen and Fernandez made an effort to keep their expressions polite but Seth's dislike of his surroundings was plain.

He looked familiar and I instinctively slouched lower in my seat. We probably played together as children, I decided. He was about the right age but as I searched my memory for whose son he might be, my mouth dried. He had fair curly hair and while I was too far away to see his eye colour, his resemblance to the Mech I had murdered was so strong I knew they had to be brothers.

My heart began an uncomfortable thump as I wondered whether his arrival in Haven was a coincidence or the result of something more sinister. If he suspected SciCorp were responsible for his brother's disappearance, he might have volunteered to come but, then again, as an Underling, he had probably just obeyed orders. Whatever the case, he had no reason to suspect me of anything, I hoped.

Micah seemed to be explaining his decision to the Mechs but seeing Lirra so close to the filth who had murdered our fathers, knotted every muscle in my body. I could not hear exactly what was said but as time went on, Micah's mystification at Adrian's continued absence became obvious.

It was not a puzzlement I shared. Iza-fungus was extremely potent and a small smear around a bowl a person favoured, ingested along with their usual breakfast, had a profoundly uncomfortable but non-life-threatening effect.

Adrian would not be leaving the latrines anytime soon and when Micah eventually sent someone to find him, Micah discovered something else I already knew: Adrian would be in no state to go anywhere for several days.

As I watched Micah mentally sift through possible replacements to accompany Lirra, I had a feeling my name was not going to be on the list. Time dragged and the Mechs' semblance of courtesy began to crack, something Micah was not blind to.

Cohen moved restlessly and as Seth's hand strayed to his weapon, I rose and threaded my way through the tables towards them.

Lirra's honeyed eyes held mine but her face was impassive and given we had grown up together, I was annoyed by how little of her feelings she showed. Refusing to play her game, I deliberately transferred my gaze to Micah.

'I am willing to accompany Lirra,' I said.

Three pairs of Mech eyes bored into me and while I kept my gaze on Micah, all my senses were trained on Seth. The Underling had definitely taken a dislike to me and I wondered whether he shared my talent for sensing things.

Micah hesitated but I held my tongue. We both knew I could go whether or not he gave his permission, but I was surprised by how much I suddenly wanted his approval.

I did not get it. Lirra ended the hiatus by rising and hefting on her pack. 'It is inconvenient Adrian is ill,' she said, and eyed the Mechs coldly. 'I certainly hope it is not something you brought with you from Station One. As time is short, I will make do with Warrain as my assistant. He has no medico training but has a little knowledge of flora and can help with any gathering I might need to do.'

I knew Lirra intended to give the impression I was nothing more than a useless boy she had been lumbered with, and that a useless boy was no threat to them, but her description rankled and I did not have to work at my sulky expression.

It would be clear to the Mechs we were both IFNO's and I hoped they thought I was motivated by an adolescent crush. I decided to add to that impression as we journeyed but, in truth, my head was full of the opportunities presented by visiting Station One.

Apart from wanting to see my mother and meet my brother or sister, and wanting them out of that dry-rat's nest, I wanted to inflict as much damage on the Mechs' cosy life-style as possible.

The Mechs already headed towards the door, eager to be gone, but as I followed with Lirra, the reality of the danger confronting us slammed home and pleasure at having evicted Adrian from the expedition evaporated.

I might just have saved his life, I realised, but my grim mood also stemmed from knowing Micah had withheld his approval of me going and that he had no such reservations about Adrian or Lirra.

I guessed the Mechs' would take the longer route down the spurs and they did. Even before the Fighting they avoided the tunnels, seeing them as stinking maggot runs that could be fallen into when the equally stinking detritus gave way. Cohen briefly introduced himself and the others to me but that was the extent of any courtesies.

We followed the Mechs who went in silence and it was a sign of their arrogance they were happy to have their backs to us. Not only were we as unimportant as the dirt beneath their feet but also too inconsequential to pose any threat.

Lirra and I did not speak either and although I glanced at her often, she kept her gaze straight ahead. Her expression in the Gathering Pod had been unreadable but it was not now. She was angry and I knew it was because Adrian had been forced to stay behind.

It confirmed her romantic feelings for him and the understanding was like a bucket of cold water tossed over my head. By the time we stopped for the night, I had convinced myself I had absolutely no need of Lirra's friendship anyway or anything else she might offer.

At the time, I was too raw to think about what that anything else might be and it was only later I realised I had assumed Lirra would always be there for me. It had never entered my head she might transfer her interest and her affections to someone else.The journey to Station One was not hard because it was all downhill along the ridge-tops but Lirra refusing to speak to me made it dreary. The Mechs were having a far more enjoyable time. As well as heading home, they were excited by the sight of the sun setting over the ocean, a view only the higher ground of the Ranges afforded.

They stared across to the other bays as they walked, and talked amongst themselves, keeping their voices low. My hearing was acute but all I learned was Seth disliked the Iron Ranges and SciCorp and having to trek beyond Station One and I had already figured that out.

We stopped for the night when the moons began to rise, their light triggering another flurry of conversation, but it was clear from what the Mechs said they had not noticed the third moon.

I resisted the urge to demonstrate any interest in the sky at all, not wanting to draw their attention to the visitor. It made me feel superior to know something they did not, but on a more practical note, I hoped the new moon might somehow disrupt the smooth workings of their comfortable, predictable lives.

The more I thought about the way they lived, the more I realised Haven would be useless to the Mechs. The Mechs were used to the automated systems of Station One, not to working out how to do things in the most rudimentary of ways.

My views were reinforced when the Mechs set camp. They had All Terrain All Weather Shelters or ATAWS, ClickHeaters that warmed food in an instant, and the sort of food packs I had concluded years before were simply a figment of my childish imagination.

I refused their offer of food on principle and was dismayed when Lirra accepted. Given her interest in nutrition, I assumed she just wanted to investigate how the food was constituted, but it still annoyed me as I munched my way through my zitin.

Lirra and I had the oiled-rast shelter sheets SciCorp developed early in our exile, but the night was mild, and we had no need of them. The Mechs set up a ClickZoneHeater anyway.

Cohen soon crawled into his ATAWS but Seth stared sullenly into space, leaving further pleasantries to Fernandez. He asked about the food sources at Station Two, what grew nearby and how it varied from season to season and interspersed his questions with descriptions of the gardens at Station One as if we merely exchanged trivial information.

I glared at Lirra, willing her to not to add to the Mechs' knowledge, but she ignored me as she had all day.

Lirra was not a fool though and simply reiterated our reliance on specific cresses, lichens and zitin the Mechs would have known about from Station One's records. Fernandez's use of the term Station Two to describe Haven also rankled.

At the time I thought it was just Mech arrogance, as if what we had built from scratch was no more special than what they had assembled from the components transported from Earth. But as I lay under the fading light of the moons, the Mechs' use of the term took on more sinister overtones, as if they saw their claim on Haven as equal to their claim on Station One.

I would have liked to test my theory on Lirra but she had slipped quickly into sleep. Fernandez and Seth did not take to their ATAWS but not because they guarded us. If either of us left without due ceremony, all they had to do was return to Station Two and procure more volunteers. Everything was simple when you had weapons.

As they sat speaking softly together, I let myself drift into the space between waking and sleeping I had created for myself as a child. I called it my Dreaming. It was not the Dreaming of my ancestors, where spirits carved out our beginnings and then rested in the land, but a place where I imagined Station One as it might have been.

In my Dreaming, Commander Andrea Thiel had slid into a gracious old age and Micah was Commander in all but name. My parents had eased back into less onerous work assisted by me and my sibling, who were both skilled and respected in our chosen fields, and the Station ran smoothly without any need for Mechs because SciCorp had the skills to deal with any contingency.

In my juvenile Dreaming, there was no place for the Mechs, as they had left no place for us. As the night drew on, the Mechs became less cautious in their speech. They probably assumed I was asleep and I nearly was until Seth's words jerked me back to full wakefulness. I remained motionless, but every nerve tingled.

'They have to know where Noah is or his body,' whispered Seth. 'They might even have murdered him!'

'We do not know he is dead,' said Fernandez, his voice a lot calmer than Seth's.

'He has been gone too long! We need to question them.'

'Our orders are to take them back. The ill are our first priority.'

'Later then,' hissed Seth.

Fernandez made no reply but given the sudden ending of the argument, I assumed he nodded. Shortly after, they turned off the Click-ZoneHeater and took to their ATAWS.

Noah. I had a name now for the dead Mech and one for his brother. Seth was not going to leave us in peace until he found out the truth and then he would execute me, murder me, I amended.

I wondered what sort of questioning Seth had in mind. Nothing gentle, I suspected, and if they threatened Lirra, I would confess.

Lirra should be safe though. They needed females if Station One were to survive and, at nineteen, Lirra was a good age to give birth, as she had sarcastically noted herself. And as an added bonus, she was also a medico.

As we went on the next day, I returned to stewing over why Micah had allowed Lirra to come in the first place. He should have sent Thi or Petar. They were both in their fifties and the brutal truth of the matter was, they had less of their lives left to live. And if one of them were killed, the other could still pass on his skills to Lirra and Adrian, and to anyone else who expressed interest in healing.

Micah claimed not to direct those of Haven and he did not, it was one of the strengths of his leadership, but such was the respect he commanded, no one ignored his advice either. So, what had he advised Lirra? To go, obviously. Like me, he had concluded there was small chance of her being killed, but I wondered whether he had considered the possibility of her being held prisoner and whether she had.

I longed to have it out with her, but it was not an exchange we could have in front of the Mechs and she continued to ignore me and the next day there was scant talk amongst the group at all.

Cohen seemed lost in thought and Seth continued to glower, leaving it to Fernandez to again attempt conversation. Lirra obliged but thankfully did not reveal anything useful.

We passed tunnel entrances without the Mechs seeming to notice and patches of lichen that purified wounds and reduced fever, and others that staved off the cold, again without them commenting.

Seth even trod in a patch of eatleaf, either because he was too ignorant to know it could keep him alive, or because he was too arrogant to value something that was not a Standard Issue food.

We spent a second night much the same as the first and came down into Sapphire Bay early the next morning without me and Lirra having exchanged a single word. I had caught more than one questioning glance pass between the Mechs and they had reason to be puzzled.

Apart from being IFNO's, two people travelling in enemy lands would have been expected to show some sort of camaraderie. The Mechs might have assumed we did not want to give information away, which was true, but a more likely explanation was we'd had a lover's tiff, which was also true in a way, despite us not being lovers.

I was angrier with Micah than with Lirra, for Lirra at least acted true to type, whereas as leader, it was Micah's responsibility to keep her safe, or perhaps he had intended to by sending Adrian with her. The realisation brought me up short.

I had taken Adrian out of the picture because I disliked his growing closeness to Lirra but now I wondered whether Micah had wanted Adrian to go, not only because he was a medico trainee, but because he was three years older, stronger, and more responsible than me.

Micah had never criticised me to my face and nor had Joseph, but the fact remained that by seventeen, most of those of Haven were busy developing useful skills. All I did was disappear into the Ranges and wander back as the mood took me, and with nothing to show for it.

My guts tightened as I contemplated the unflattering view the more senior members of SciCorp probably held of me, and Fernandez dropping back to walk beside me as we neared Station One, did not help.

'Do you have family here?' he asked.

'My mother,' I said shortly, keeping my gaze on Station One's voltaged fence, 'and a brother or sister I have never met.'

'And your mother's name is?'

The way the Mech asked it was like an interrogation and I considered not answering. Yet if I were to see my mother again he would soon know who she was anyway, so it seemed childish to remain silent.

'Parri,' I said. 'When you lot killed my father, my mother stayed behind at Station One because she was pregnant. It gave my brother or sister a better chance at life than going into the Ranges where there was nothing.'

I made no attempt to moderate my belligerence and I half expected the Mech to sling something back, but his expression remained bland. 'We are to go to Commander Singh first,' was all he said.

I had planned to stride back into Station One with my head thrown back and my shoulders squared but as we neared the Station I simply stared. It looked the same as my childhood memories but also different and it was certainly smaller.

I mentally checked off what I saw against my recollections: the men's pod, the women's pod, the couples' pods, the instructional pods, the pods for cooking and eating, the Infirmary and storage pods, the work pods, and beyond those, the gardens and nursery, the greenhouses and stores, the machine and tool pods.

Children played as they did at Haven but the adults stopped in their tracks. Seth's hand was back near his weapon and he swaggered as if we were his prisoners, captured through some personal act of bravery. He was half right, I concluded sourly, we were prisoners, but conveniently, had come of our own volition. The understanding kicked my brain into gear and my senses and I started to concentrate.

The hum told me the voltaged fence was still live and suggested the Mechs' still had trouble with shadcats, and the unaltered configuration of the Station told me the Mechs had failed to develop anything new and that told me they were not likely to respond quickly to any new challenge.

Nor was Singh the name of the man Joseph said commanded the Mechs. Maybe the man who had led the Mechs' murderous rampage had died, or retired, or sunk into an arrash stupor. I tried to remember where the weapons store was and whether the ammunition was stored separately but was swamped by too many other memories. The last time I had been here, the air had been thick with blood and the sound of women weeping.

Lirra's tension was palpable and our eyes met for the first time since leaving Haven. In different ways, we had both been orphaned that day and now were back among those who had robbed us of our families. Even if our Mech guards had been absent, I doubt we would have spoken. There were no words for the horror that had unfolded.

'Commander Singh has had responsibility for Station One for the last four years,' said Cohen, as we threaded our way between pods.

My thoughts whirred. That meant Singh had taken over shortly after the slaughter. But was that a good or a bad sign? No party of Mechs had appeared in the Ranges to offer apologies and the key to Station One's gate so maybe the change resulted from some internal power struggle. Having murdered and expelled SciCorp, the Mechs might have turned on each other. If they had, I hoped the death rate had been high.

Cohen knocked on the door of a small pod and then ushered us in. He did not follow and nor did Fernandez or Seth, but I barely noticed. There were several Mechs at work inside but Singh was easy to pick.

His desk was bigger than the others and his chair as grand as those used by the pilots on the Settler Ship. He rose but it was a struggle and once he was upright I saw why. He leaned on two metal-topped sticks.

'Welcome to Station One, members of SciCorp,' he said, 'or more properly, welcome back to Station One.'

He had done us the courtesy of standing and his greeting held neither irony nor sarcasm, which was surprising enough, but my mystification deepened as I watched him manoeuvre himself awkwardly around the desk. His legs were stiff and he dragged his right foot.

'You can wait outside,' he said to the Mechs who worked nearby.

One of them was clearly reluctant. 'Commander, I think it would be unwise …'

'I do not think our guests will attack me, at least not yet,' Singh told him ironically.

The door clicked shut behind me as they exited and only then did my tension ease enough for me to focus fully on Singh.

Apart from his reliance on sticks, the most notable thing about him was the dark red material he wore on his head like a complicated hat. It obscured his hair and, although his skin was smooth, his brows were grey-flecked. He was darker than Lirra and me but no IFNO and I decided he probably came from the same place in Asia as Vijay, SciCorp's physicist.

No doubt Lirra's sharp eyes were taking in the same detail as mine and Singh waited for us to finish our appraisals.

'Please sit,' he said, and gestured to the newly vacated chairs.

Lirra took the chair closest to him and I took one further back. It gave me a view of the door and of the yard beyond the window.

Singh lowered himself painfully down onto a third chair and it was no surprise to me Lirra was first to speak or what she said. 'You were attacked by a shadcat?'

'In a way,' he murmured, and his gaze sharpened on me. 'You are a medico?'

I shook my head and he swivelled to Lirra. 'Then you are.'

'I have training,' said Lirra, 'and so volunteered to come. You understand why it was unwise for SciCorp to send our most experienced medicos?'

'Yet,' amended Singh, and my tension ratcheted up again. There was no mistaking the threat despite his mild tone. I glanced around for a weapon but there were none. The room was like a sophisticated version of Joseph's record pod.

'We do not keep weapons here,' said Singh, his dark eyes on mine. My face warmed but I refused to drop my gaze. 'So,' he continued, 'SciCorp has granted me a medico in training and a ...?' I said nothing, and his tone became bantering. 'Brother? Lover? Kinsman?' Still I said nothing and his voice grew serious again. 'I am guessing you have family here then.'

'A mother and a brother or sister,' I confirmed. 'My mother stayed after you killed my father. She was pregnant.'

'So, you have come back to see them?'

'Yes.' It was the simplest answer but not entirely true given my want to separate Lirra and Adrian, and deal the Mechs some sort of blow.

'Your mother is Caucasian?'

It was an odd question and it put me on the back foot. I had never known an IFNO who was so-called full-blood, nor anyone else for that matter. Earth's stocks of blacks, whites and yellows had interbred for thousands of years before the Settler Ships classified people by the DNA in their spit. The whole ethnic quota system was more of a political game than any serious attempt to populate new Sats with a representational sample of the best Earth has to offer.

Despite the white blood Lirra and I carried, it was hard to confuse what we were. We both had darker skins and black curly hair, although Lirra's eyes were lighter than mine. And we saw the world around us differently to those of other blood-mixes or felt it differently, as Lirra would say.

'My mother is IFNO as was my father, as is the brother or sister I have never met,' I said.

Singh made his way awkwardly back behind his desk and stared down intently, probably at a data-slab, although I could not see.

I had heard Joseph bemoan the loss of such things as he laboured to prepare his rast bark paper and inks. Singh was obviously checking the veracity of my claims and I saw his mouth tighten but he said nothing, just hauled himself painfully back to the seat in front of us.

'Station One's records tell me I am most likely in the company of Lirra Gnattarre, daughter of SciCorp Officers Woorin Gnattarre and Pindan Gnattarre, and Warrain Gnarraway son of SciCorp Officers Uwan Gnarraway and Parri Gnarraway.'

'Correct,' I clipped out.

'Woorin Gnattarre died during the fighting. His wife Pindan re-partnered and bore two children, sons now aged five and four,' went on Singh. 'Uwan Gnarraway died during the fighting as well, and his wife Parri died from complications suffered during childbirth. The child died also.'

There was absolute silence. My mother and brother or sister had died because the Mechs had killed or expelled the medicos. There was no mother to be rescued and no sibling to come to know and there never had been. Lirra's gaze met and held mine. She had two brothers as well as a mother here, whereas I had no one.

And as we stared at each other, we both knew I should never have come.

9

Singh allowed me time to just sit and I should have seen that as a good sign. It meant the man had some compassion in him but I was barely aware of the room, let alone him. I had grown up nurturing the belief that, one day I would return in triumph and reclaim my family and now that belief had been exposed for what it was: the hollow imaginings of a powerless boy.

To make matters worse, Lirra, who had chosen to leave, not only had a mother here but two brothers as well. I did not begrudge her the good fortune of a family, but her gain intensified my loss.

It was Lirra who eventually broke the silence. 'Tell me about the illness at Station One,' she said.

I heard the Mech Commander respond and for a while their voices went to and fro on the edges of my consciousness. I knew I should attend but it was Lirra who was the expert in interpreting symptoms and concocting medicines.

My skill lay in knowing the dips and slopes the suited certain plants and in sensing the subtle differences between them that resulted from variations in moisture, sunlight and soil.

At some point, I became aware their speech had stopped and Lirra had risen and I stumbled to my feet.

'Tom Fernandez will take you to the Infirmary and provide you with any further information you require,' said Singh. 'We will speak again later.' He barked an order, making me jump, and our escorts reappeared. Singh had obviously decided we posed no threat because he dismissed Cohen and Seth with a wave of his hand, and we followed Fernandez back out into the yard.

Lirra and Fernandez made their way between the pods and as I tagged along behind, my numbness slowly dissipated, and I became aware of the sun's warm rays on my skin and of a distant hiss.

The sea, I realised. How often had I slipped away to watch the surge and suck of the waves up and down the beach and been reprimanded by Commander Thiel, especially in the early days when the extent of the shadcats' threat was unknown. I had loved the sea's openness then and I loved it now.

When it became apparent shadcats shunned the sea, SciCorp added the coast around Station One to their schedule of studies. As a child, I worked alongside biologists as they analysed the comings and goings of shoals, their breeding grounds, and habitats. Anders, in particular, encouraged me and I sensed even then how keen he was I continue his work, and I may have, had his work not ended with his life on the day of the Fighting.

The Infirmary looked exactly as I remembered but I was seized with panic as I followed Fernandez in. What if one of the deadly diseases that had afflicted the Ancients lurked inside? A plague or pox that Lirra and I were going to be deliberately infected with and sent back to Haven to spread?

My panic was momentary. It was quiet inside and Fernandez led us past empty pallets to a partitioned area at the far end of the pod. Several young women sat at a desk and an older woman sat beside one of the pallets in a curtained alcove. She looked up as we came in, her face hungry for hope.

The pallet held the shape of a small boy and my guts churned as empathy mixed with a long stew of bitterness. Lirra suffered no such qualms. She went straight to the bed, laid her hand across the boy's brow, and leaned close to check his breathing. Then she launched into a series of questions that the women at the desk and the one at the bed—who I guessed was the child's mother—answered in turn.

Fernandez's hard gaze was on me and it was obvious he saw me as a threat. My face probably betrayed more of my feelings than I wanted, but even had my expression been docile or sycophantic, my age and sex flagged me.

The worst violence of the Fighting had been carried out by younger Mechs and these men were now Fernandez's age.

In one of Joseph's many warnings disguised as rambling stories, he had described how young male mammals on Earth formed their own groups where they tested themselves against each other in play-fights, then in contests, then in fights to the death. Earth's history was littered with accounts of millions of young men formed into armies to murder millions of other young men formed into armies, he said.

At the time, I had seen no connection between such stories and my determination to avenge my father's death, but I did now and Fernandez's animosity was abruptly the least of my problems.

As I stared down at the sick boy and at his mother, her face pale with worry, the black and white of right and wrong, of justice and revenge, merged into a blur of grey that left me utterly confused. It was easier to hate from a distance, I discovered, than to hate close-up.

Lirra took the boy's pulse, looked into his eyes, and checked his tongue, all simple things the Mechs had probably done. They might not be medicos, but they had the data computes and slabs with everything imaginable encoded on them and they had all the SI medicines. In fact, it was hard to understand why they needed us at all.

Lirra turned to the woman at the desk and rattled off another set of questions but it was Fernandez who answered most of them. He was surprisingly precise as to when the sickness started, who had been affected, what treatments had been tried, and the results.

It was at odds with the picture I had built of the Mechs being rough and ready men, skilled at building and maintenance and seeking pleasure, but not much else. Then again, a lot can change in five years or as I later realised, as a boy grows up.

The Mechs had to compensate for the gap left by SciCorp just as we had to fill the hole left by them and by Station One. Of course, the split had been the Mechs' choice and their loss far less until now.

We had to build our own pods, find our own food, provide our own tools to continue our studies. But as I listened to Fernandez clip out responses to Lirra's questions, I realised it was easier to build a shelter than uncover the reason for an illness and devise a cure.

It had taken the Ancients thousands of years to discover which plants cured and which plants killed, let alone the existence of bacteria and viruses. SciCorp carried a lot of this information in their heads and had added to it since, especially about Imago's medicinal resources.

The Mechs had the data preloaded on their systems but information alone was not enough. You had to understand what to do with it.

For once we were in a more powerful position than they were. All I had to do was work out what the crad to do about it.

There were three more children beyond the curtain, two boys and a little girl and, as we trooped from one to the other, the full implications of what happened sank in. Micah said there had been deaths and I wondered if they had been children too. I shuddered. What would happen if the same sickness struck Haven?

Our numbers were already low. To lose children would be catastrophic. The Mechs' numbers were probably low too, I realised. No wonder they turned their eyes towards the Ranges.

But it was not just about numbers but about ending children's shouts and children's laughter and with it, any hope of a future. I thought of the brother or sister I had never known and forced my attention back to Lirra.

The Mech and the women stared at her too, but unlike me, they did not know what they looked at. Lirra's face was impassive except for a slight quirk to her mouth which meant deep thinking and puzzlement in equal measure.

As we moved away from the last child, a girl of about four, Fernandez bent and kissed her on the forehead. It was only then I noticed the resemblance and realised just how high the stakes were.

If the Mechs suspected we were not doing everything in our power to save their children, they would ensure we did, and that could mean taking and killing hostages or taking Petar and Thi. There was nothing to stop Mechs harvesting Haven for whatever resources they needed, human or otherwise.

Medicos were an obvious choice, but why not take our botanists to improve the Mechs' yields, or our geologists to find minerals for black trade. They might even steal our children if theirs were wiped out.

I rolled my shoulders to ease their tension but the set of Lirra's mouth told me she focussed only on the problem at hand. 'Has anything changed at the Station?' she asked.

'In what way?' It was Fernandez again, jumping in before the women could speak.

'Anything. The taste of the water, how your food crops blossom and grow, the hardness of the ground …' Lirra trailed off. I was relieved she had not mentioned the moon. It would already be subtly altering Imago's gravitational fields, although how that could cause sickness was beyond me.

'Any statistically significant variations would have been reported but I will have the data rechecked.'

Lirra and I looked at each other blankly and it took me a minute to work out what Fernandez meant. Robbed of the automated systems Station One relied on, we judged the health of our food stocks by their taste and smell and texture.

We did as the Ancients had done and got our hands dirty, but the Mechs were reliant on their systems and I suddenly saw the risk. If whatever caused the sickness did not disrupt designated parameters, the systems would ignore it.

I thought of how the moons affected lin-lichen. Eat it under a waning moon and you would swear you ate the deliciously aromatic sour-lichen. Eat it when the moons' waxed and you would be firm friends with the latrines for days.

And a change that was subtle would show up in the children first! Their smaller bodies were less able to deal with pathogenic assault and their rapid cell division caused by their growing also made them more vulnerable.

Lirra seemed to be thinking along the same lines. 'Do the children have the same diet as the adults?'

'Their diets conform to the relevant code,' said the woman at the desk indignantly.

'You think there is a problem with our food sources that has shown up in the young first?' asked Fernandez. He was quicker on the uptake than the woman but he had a lot more riding on the outcome.

'All four children are severely anaemic,' said Lirra, 'but I presume your tests have told you that.'

Fernandez's gaze swung to the woman at the desk and she shook her head. 'The blood tests are normal.'

'Their gums and lower lids show anaemia. I need to see the gardens,' said Lirra, and strode out.

10

I knew from Joseph that all Stations, no matter which Sat they were on, had the same Food Generation Systems or FGS's, just as they had the same number and type of pods in the same configuration, and that even the pods' internal fit-outs were identical.

Space Corp claimed this resulted in maximum efficiency but my father had muttered something about cookie-cutter imaginations. By the time I understood what the term meant, he had taken a blast in the lung and drowned in his own blood.

When we had started to build Haven, we had marked out a replica of Station One but one day Judith asked why Haven had to have squares when so much of Imago was rounded. It was such an odd question I remember that work actually stopped.

No one could see any reason not to have curves either, especially as they did replicate the tunnel entrances, the striate-filled valleys, and even the shape of the Iron Ranges, and now as I stared at the rectangular plots of vegetables and treefruit, I was glad we had created something new, in Lirra's terms, something more Imagoan.

It had taken time to find the right mix of companion plantings to keep the leaf-eaters at bay, attract the right moth-pollinators, and to selectively breed plants so those like zitin produced higher yields. And while our botanists and chemists had worked away on this, we subsisted on a limited range of cresses and lichens that, while nutritionally sound, were as boring as all crad.

The Mechs enjoyed a far greater variety of food and I stared at the neat plots of glossy-leaved vegetables and orange and yellow treefruit enviously. Explorer Ships sampled each newly discovered Sat and Space Corp engineered food plants tailored to the Sat's environment.

Some of these plants self-perpetuated and needed no external pollination while others mimicked existing Imagoan flora to attract pollinators. The Mechs did not need to labour as we did at Haven because the Station's automated systems delivered set amounts of nourishment and water.

Now I wondered whether this was a weakness. If something had changed, plants engineered in another time and place to suit the old Imago, might not be able to adjust to suit the new one.

I followed Lirra as she wandered between the plots. Here and there she turned over leaves to examine their underside or dug her thumbnail into a vein and touched the rich ooze to her tongue. I simply let the scents wash over me as I considered the colour of their leaves and how each plant sat in relation to another.

I saw nothing amiss but that did not mean things were fine either. The whole set up was unnatural and what I had envied just a short while before began to jar.

That Lirra asked Fernandez whether anything had changed, probably meant she could not see anything wrong either. It would have been simple had she found some noxious type of leaf-eater at work the Mechs could eliminate and so have no reason to ever visit Haven again.

Lirra had stopped and stood hands on hips as she contemplated the fence. 'Had any trouble with shadcats recently?' she asked.

I knew enough of Lirra to know she bought time and I kept my face impassive.

'Not shadcats,' said Fernandez, 'but there have been more maggots than at any time since Station One was established. They are heading into the Ranges. I am surprised you have not seen them at Station Two.'

Lirra tensed but kept her gaze on the fence. 'Do you observe the Protection Zone?' she asked abruptly.

'That was a SciCorp regulation.'

Lirra's eyes blazed and it was my turn to tense. 'That was a Space Corp regulation to protect indigenous life-forms!'

'You are not here to reimpose SciCorp's authority,' said Fernandez coldly. 'You are here to find a cure for our children. Have you found anything wrong with the food crops?'

'Not yet but there is a malaise here,' said Lirra, her words deliberately ambiguous. I was just glad she had not used the word rotten. I was cowardly enough to want to get out of Station One alive.

We moved into the orchards but whereas before Lirra had strolled amongst the food plants, now she strode. I was surprised at the depth of her anger at the Mechs' refusal to honour the Protection Zones. It was hardly news. A group of men who plied their trades for the highest coin were unlikely to give a crad about protecting a planet's flora and fauna.

The influence of Earth's pressure groups had waxed and waned over the years but there had been periods when they had forced Space Corp to introduce all sorts of regulations to protect newly discovered Sats, particularly their sentient life forms.

Debates raged over what constituted 'sentient', especially when a Sat was stuffed with Designated Essential Materials, then the debate shifted to the 'responsible harvesting of resources for the greater good of humanity.' It was a moot point anyway. The galaxy was a big place for the Trad ships to hide in even before the Interstellar Judiciary ships had disappeared.

Lirra held her silence as she strode about the orchard and so did I despite a tang in the air that set my teeth on edge. 'I need to speak to Warrain alone,' she said finally.

'What is there to be said that cannot be said publicly?' asked Fernandez, his face heavy with suspicion.

'There are many things,' said Lirra, and when Fernandez's expression remained unchanged, added: 'I have one set of skills and Warrain has another. I want to see if his feelings match mine and it is a discussion best had without the weapons of those who murdered our fathers at our hearts.'

The strength of Lirra's anger again took me aback. It had always been Lirra who had insisted we move on rather than dwell on the past, but now our positions seemed to have reversed. I expected some angry response from the Mech, especially since his daughter seemed to be among the ill, but there was not one.

'The past cannot be undone,' he said, 'but we hope for a better future. We will meet again at dusk. Until then have your time and your privacy, but there will be eyes on you. While the past cannot be undone, it is not forgotten.'

'Crad-head,' muttered Lirra, as he strode off. 'He makes it sound like we started the Fighting, not his lot with their weapons and greed for arrash.'

'Joseph reckons people make-up stories about their past to justify whatever they did,' I said. 'I suppose the Mechs are a case in point.' Lirra continued to glare and I tried again. 'I think that last little girl in the Infirmary was his daughter or maybe even his sister. If so, Fernandez's got a lot vested in us coming up with a fast cure and in not leaving without proper farewells.'

Lirra's honey eyes came to mine. 'I am sorry about your mother, Warrain, and about your brother or sister. And I am sorry my mother was so quick to forgive.' I resisted the urge to reach for her, knowing we were watched, and the silence stretched. 'Did you sense anything amiss in the gardens?' she asked.

'Yes. Did you?'

She nodded. 'But do not ask me what. If they have tested everything there is to test, why should we trust our skins?'

'Black fella knowing,' I said, with an attempt at humour. 'Our ancestors used the same tricks to help the first white fellas find food when they were starving.'

'More fool them,' said Lirra, but her expression eased. We started back through the pods aware that Mechs shadowed us. They kept their distance, as Fernandez promised, but we kept our voices low.

'They would have tested everything in the gardens and orchards,' I said. 'Whatever it is must be new and so outside their systems' settings.'

'Or too subtle to be picked up,' said Lirra. 'And remember the Mechs do not have our skills.'

'Their systems are pretty foolproof though,' I felt bound to point out. 'Sure, we could use them more skilfully than this mob of Mechs, but the readings should still show whether their water, soil, food and bodily functions are affected. And the Mechs have had five years to practise without us around.'

Lirra said nothing and we came to a stop at the station fence. The sea's voice sang in my ears and we needed no discussion about where we wanted to head.

'We are going to the shore,' I yelled back to our escort. The information must have been passed along the line for the gate swung open and we exited and turned along the narrow sandy path we had last taken as children.

It was pretty much overgrown, which surprised me. As I had stared down from the Tors, I had imagined the Mechs swimming and lazing on the beach, but it did not look like anyone had used the path in years. Our hungry gazes took in the sprawls of salt-pea and delicately tinted pink-eye, its blooms starting to close for the day, and then the great sweep of the ocean came into view and we stopped.

I was vaguely aware our Mech escort had stopped too but my throat had tightened and I sensed Lirra's tension as she stood beside me. This had been a happy place where we had played with the other children of Station One, SciCorp and Mech alike which, in one bloody afternoon, had all been swept away.

'How can everything be the same and yet so utterly different?' murmured Lirra.

I took her hand and brought it to my lips. 'It is good to be here again, despite everything. Let us go for a walk,' I said, and self-conscious suddenly, dropped her hand.

We turned along the shore and as our instincts kicked in again, looked for something, anything, that might explain the illness at Station One. The shore had the same shells, tosses of weed, and stands of palms I remembered. Nothing looked odd or out of place.

'Do you think the maggots have something to do with the sickness?' asked Lirra, after a while.

'Anything is possible,' I said, but I could not imagine how the maggots could cause illness and death at Station One, and even if they had somehow fouled the water or food supplies, the Station's systems would have picked it up.

The possibility the maggots were deliberately doing something came to mind, but I dismissed the idea. If the maggots had some sort of secret weapon, they would have used it well before now.

We settled on the sand and gazed at the sea in silence. If we had not had the Mechs glaring at us from across the way, I would have taken Lirra's hand again, but their animosity buffeted my skin like the cooling breeze. It was almost dusk, which was all the time Fernandez had given us, and yet Lirra and I had not got beyond agreeing that we felt uneasy.

'You do not think the maggots are causing any of this, do you?' said Lirra. 'And if it is not the maggots, that leaves the third moon as the main suspect.' She kept her eyes on the water as she spoke, and I was careful not to glance skywards too.

'It might be something else,' I said, 'but it would be a giant of a coincidence.'

'Coincidences are pretty common,' she said acerbically, 'but let us assume for argument's sake that it is the third moon. Its pull will certainly alter the tides but could also alter other things more subtly.'

'You mean turn the Mechs into lunatics?' I quipped. 'We do not need another moon for that.'

'Apparently, Earth's moon really did affect people's mental state,' said Lirra, in her best medico voice.

'But not their physical state, at least not enough to make them sick or kill them,' I replied.

'No, but there were lots of flora and fauna on Earth whose growth and fertility were controlled by the moon, and there was only one moon there whereas Imago now has three.'

'So, you think it is to do with the third moon?' I asked.

'Yes, or it could just be a coincidence,' she said, with a crooked smile.

'Or magic,' I added, with a lightness I did not feel.

'Same thing,' said Lirra, her gaze on the dunes. They were strewn with sea wrack but when we had played slide on them as children, they had been high and dry.

'The last tide was big,' I said.

Lirra nodded. 'I wonder if the Mechs have noticed.'

'I doubt it. Given the state of the path, I do not think they come here very often.'

'Too busy plundering the Protection Zone,' said Lirra sourly. The Mechs were making their way along the beach towards us and we rose and brushed the sand off ourselves. 'We are going to have to come up with something soon,' she whispered, as our escort approached.

'We are running out of time.'

Instead of taking us back to Singh's pod for another round of inter-rogation, our escort took us to the dining pod and led us through the seated Mechs to Singh's table. While my skin had sensed something subtly amiss in the gardens, it positively shrieked warning at me now.

Silence followed in our wake and Seth glowered at us from a table of equally hostile young Mechs. I kept my head up and my gaze straight ahead and I was proud that Lirra was unbowed too.

Joseph had once told me that, back on Earth, pretending not to be scared was called whistling in the dark, and I reckon Lirra and I were whistling at the top of our lungs. But it was only after we sat down I realised her fear did not flow from the same place as mine: the male Mechs in the room, but from those seated to Singh's right.

It was Lirra's mother Pindan, I realised in shock, and the two lit-tle boys beside her could only be Lirra's brothers. The most generous interpretation of Singh's arrangement of so public a reunion was he wanted to make amends for the Mechs' bloody past, but he might also want to give Lirra a greater incentive to find the cause of the sickness.

After all, if she did not, her brothers might succumb. Then again, it might be a ploy to prompt Lirra to fall sobbing into her mother's arms and, in doing so, reveal everything she knew about Haven. If Singh's motivation had been any of these things, he was to be disap-pointed.

Lirra nodded to her mother and after a brief glance at her broth-ers, turned her face away. No such inhibitions impeded me and I stared at them. My memories of Pindan were of a jokey, carefree woman who raced Lirra and me along the beach, or prepared lis-juice for us so fresh it bubbled on our tongues.

But any resemblance to that woman was fleeting. Her hair was grey and her face deeply lined. I nodded to her but she had eyes only for Lirra, her gaze so hungry I was embarrassed by Lirra's reaction and had to resist kicking her under the table.

Lirra had been fourteen when she had stolen away with us and I had thought it was the kind of spit-in-your-face bravado Lirra was famous for. But now as I ate the sweet rich food I had not tasted for years, and watched Pindan watch Lirra, I wondered if there was more to it.

Singh had said the boys were four and five and that meant the elder must have been conceived directly after the Fighting. A shiver ran over my skin as I wondered whether the boys knew how Pindan's first husband had died and that they had a sister growing up in the Ranges.

And if they did know, what tale had been spun to them? That SciCorp had started the Fighting? That we were dangerous criminals who were expelled for the boys' safety? That we were still a threat?

The boys' curiosity did not last long and, as they tucked into their meal, I shifted my attention to the rest of the Mechs and calculated who was old enough to be murderers, who their children were, and who had been born since.

Given Lirra's brothers' ages, Pindan had not wasted much time in mourning and the boys' light skins told me their father was not an IFNO. Not that I could add that to Pindan's sins given the only IFNO men had been my and Lirra's fathers.

I knew Singh watched me as I reconnoitred the room and I let my gaze slide over him to those seated to his other side and noticed the young women for the first time. For a wild moment, I thought my sibling had survived after all, and that Singh pulled the same stunt on me as he pulled on Lirra, but logic told me the girls were no relation.

Singh was up to something but I still could not help but stare at them. All the girls at Haven, apart from Lirra, had been born there. I had seen their mothers grow big, sensed the tension in members of SciCorp as their pregnancies drew to their conclusions, and felt the excitement as they laboured in the rudimentary Infirmary under the expert care of Thy and Petar.

Then the women were out and about again with small bundles slung across their fronts. The bundles elongated and tottered about and then joined the other children in their shrill games.

I was seventeen then and the oldest of the girls conceived at Haven less than five which meant it would be another eleven or twelve years before I could be more than a friend to any of them and that was only if they chose me from all the other men of my age.

The Mech girls stared at me as much as I stared at them and heat stirred, deep in my guts. Singh's gaze remained on me and anger surged as well as lust and I managed to drag my eyes away.

'Allow me to introduce you,' he said.

'There is no need.'

His smile was oddly sympathetic. 'There is no trap intended, Warrain,' he said. 'I know from what occurred five years ago there are few women of your age in Station Two. I thought you might enjoy meeting some.'

'Like Lirra enjoyed meeting the mother and brothers you robbed her of?' My voice was strident and any semblance of conversation in the pod ceased.

'I thought she would like to see them, yes,' said Singh.

'In such a public place?'

Singh opened his mouth to reply but Lirra got in first. 'Ignore him, Warrain. It is just mind games.'

Again, I expected Singh to be angry, but his expression remained mild. 'Finish your meals. There will be time for talking later.'

We ate in silence, the food sweet, creamy and smooth, the kind I vaguely remembered from my childhood. Haven's foods were less strongly flavoured and more fibrous and after our expulsion, I dreamed of the confections served up on Station One's registered holy days. But now I found the flavours of even these everyday foods almost sickly.

Lirra only picked at her meal but I guessed its sweetness had little to do with her lack of appetite. Her brothers might be tucking into their food like there was no tomorrow but Pindan's gaze on her was unremitting.

A Mech set a jug on the table and my mouth watered as I smelled lis-juice. I poured myself some and the beaker was almost to my lips when I stopped. The sense of wrongness about it was faint but undeniable and I set the beaker down again.

I glanced at Lirra to see if she noticed anything amiss but she stared morosely into space and the dishes were being cleared before anyone spoke again and then it was Singh.

'I am aware Lirra is training to be a medico,' he said, 'but not what you are pursuing.'

I resisted the urge to agree that Singh was indeed correct in not knowing what I pursued but had already shown myself to be churlish and I did not want to strengthen the impression. 'Nothing yet,' I muttered.

'So how do you spend your days?'

'There is no lack of work at Haven,' I said. 'It does not have the benefits of systems delivered from Earth.'

'And assembled here and maintained far from external help,' said Singh, alluding to the Mechs' skills and labour.

I said nothing. It was true the Mechs had assembled the systems and did maintain them and SciCorp had benefitted from them, as indeed the Mechs had. But Station One and its sister Stations elsewhere in the galaxy had not been established to keep the Mechs' in work. They had been established to add to Earth's understanding and knowledge or so their enormous expense had been sold to the good citizens of Earth.

It was only later I fully understood what my parents had muttered about when they had been angry, that Earth was only interested in extracting DEMs, and that SciCorp's investigations were simply a means to that end.

It was fully dark by the time we accompanied Singh back to his pod. Seth followed with another young Mech Singh briefly introduced as Dieter. He looked as hostile as Seth and I did not bother to hide my feelings either. Singh's pain seemed to have increased during the day and it was slow going, so I had plenty of time to enjoy Dieter and Seth's glares.

The two moons were close to full, but I was careful to keep my gaze on Singh's shadow as it heaved itself over the ground. The yard was not the rammed earth of Haven but the standard issue synth-turf that, according to their sales blurb, was 'sealing the galaxy one Station at a time'.

I found it strange that the marketing jingle should come back to me now. Maybe it was the hollow sound of our footfalls that triggered the memory, but it also unleashed less welcome memories of the crack that weapons fire made as it glanced off.

Cold sweat started down my back and my knotted muscles were not helped by the Mechs' aggression behind me or by the voltaged fence that hemmed us in and prevented escape. Lirra did not speak either or look my way; she simply took my hand and locked our fingers so that her palm pressed hard against mine. Lirra's touch calmed and disturbed me, but I resisted the urge to pull away, not wanting to give the Mechs something else to sneer at.

Lirra and I spent a lot of time together growing up and not just because we were IFNO's. As the only girl child in Haven, Lirra had been forced to choose a male playmate and she had chosen me.

Our friendship had survived the confusion of puberty and the years that lead up to her choice to be a medico, and the understanding she had now left me behind hit me afresh and threw me further off balance. I staggered and Singh came to a stop and leaned heavily on his sticks as if he needed a break.

'It is not easy to return to a place of so many bad memories,' he said softly, his gaze on the fence as if he commented only on that. 'And it is especially hard for an IFNO male on the verge of initiation or has the ceremony already taken place?'

Lirra and I froze but for different reasons. 'What do you know of IFNO's?' she asked.

'More than the average Mech,' said Singh dryly, and then his gaze swung to our escort. 'Perhaps we will continue our conversation in my pod,' he murmured.

We held our silence until Singh was ensconced behind his desk and Seth and Dieter cooled their heels outside, but Singh's behaviour puzzled me. He acted as if Seth and Dieter were his enemies too.

'I have often thought that one of Space Corp's better decisions was to include IFNO's in the Settler Programs,' he said, keeping his voice low despite the closed door. 'Those of First Nations heritage seem to remember better than the rest of us what it is to live in harmony with the land, and what it is to lose it, sensibilities important to the protection of sentient species on new Sats.'

'Sentient species?' I repeated gracelessly. 'I thought you Mechs had bled them all to death.'

Singh's face tightened. 'Do you recall who led the Mechtechnicians in the Fighting, Warrain?' I shrugged. 'It was Leading Mechtechnician Jacob McKenzie.'

It took me a moment to pick up on the name. 'You mean Seth's father?'

'Seth and his twin Noah's, who happens to be missing at the moment.'

I felt as if my guilt were branded on my face in white-hot letters and took the opportunity to brush some remnant sand from my trouser legs.

'So, what happened to Jacob McKenzie?' asked Lirra, her voice as tight as my chest.

'Things rolled along for a while because his links to the Trads and disregard for the Protection Zones meant he provided what his fellow addicts craved. But even unaffected by arrash, Jacob was a hard man to reason with. You were either for Jacob or against him. There was nothing in between.'

Lirra's face was strangely frozen and it was my turn to fill the silence. 'So, you had Jacob McKenzie removed,' I said. Singh's warning glance at the door reminded me to lower my voice and I obliged. 'I imagine he did not go quietly,' I muttered, and then understanding dawned as my gaze came to rest on Singh's sticks.

'There was another fight,' confirmed Singh, 'but this time there were enough of us free of arrash to remember why we joined the Settler Program in the first place and to remember all the excellent reasons why we did not want to slide into chaos.

'The Station's systems are robust but even they will not work forever without proper maintenance and that is if they are not sabotaged. We secured the weapons first or so we thought.'

'You were shot?' asked Lirra. Her medico training had kicked in and there was life in her face again.

'Several times and five others wounded. There were seven deaths.'

'Your side or theirs?' asked Lirra.

Singh's eyes glittered. 'There can be no more "sides", Lirra; there can only be us.'

'The Mechs you mean.'

'I mean SciCorp and the Mechtechnicians. When Space Corp set up its Settler Programs, it got the balance right. The Mechtechnicians were included because they had the skills to provide and maintain the Stations and all the other things SciCorp needed to conduct their research. If SciCorp had not been expelled, I would be in less pain now,' he finished grimly.

'Expelled is a bit too clean a word for it, Singh,' I said. 'Murdered and thrown out into nothingness would be a more accurate description. How long has Jacob been gone? He is dead I presume?'

'Jacob has not been Commander for over four years. And no, he is not dead. He is under arrest in the Confinement Pod until an IJ ship collects him. Space Corp has been notified.'

Lirra actually laughed. 'And their response was?'

'We are still waiting for it.'

'Is that why Seth hates you?' I asked.

'Seth hates everyone,' said Singh. 'Like a lot of young men of his age.'

His gaze was hard on me but I ignored his unsubtle message. 'But surely Jacob has still got supporters,' I said, 'who are not content to have him locked up and you in charge?'

'He has some sympathisers,' conceded Singh. 'But once the arrash dried up and they literally came to their senses, they realised Station One was not sustainable unless they did what they signed up to do.'

'But if Station One fails, all you have to do is come and throw us out of Haven.'

'That was put as an argument,' said Singh. 'Why bother maintaining Station One when we can simply take Station Two? But Haven, as you call it, would be a far more difficult Station to keep functioning and impossible if our Mechtechnicians remain arrash-affected.

'Station One was shipped from Earth and is a product of Space Corp's considerable expertise, whereas Station Two was, by necessity, constructed from what could be scrounged from Imago. Without having seen it, I am presuming your living conditions are far less comfortable than those here.'

My throat was so tight I could not speak. I had hardly demonstrated prescience by predicting the Mechs would take Haven if they felt like it but that only laziness had prevented it, added to my fury.

'Why are you telling us all this?' demanded Lirra.

'Because, as I said before, there can be no more "them and us", no more "Mechs" and "Psycho Corps". If we are to carry out the mission Space Corp charged us with, we must work together, as Space Corp intended.'

We both gaped at Singh and it was Lirra who recovered quickest.

'Surely you are not suggesting SciCorp comes back to Station One?'

'Not immediately nor that SciCorp shares Station Two. But we need to work towards reunification.'

'We do not need you or Station One anymore,' I ground out. 'It is you who need us.'

Singh eyed me in his usual calm manner. 'Five years is not very long to test your rudimentary systems against what Imago might throw up, Warrain. The Data Pod contained detailed analyses of Imago's systems and, despite their loss, Station One's systems were constructed to adjust to any future challenges, probably unlike Station Two's.

'As for your skills in medicines and plants, you are quite right. But what sickens our children might be the beginning of what will soon sicken yours, and both our populations are vulnerable to extinction if we lose the next generation. There is also the matter of the Medico's Oath. You are bound to offer cure where illness exists.'

'It is a bit late to talk about ethics,' I began, but then Lirra cut in.

'You are quite right, Commander, that an illness in either place could spread but in error if you believe we medicos need reminding of our obligations.' There was a prickly pause. 'But given what has happened, I do not see how those of us at Haven and those of you at Station One can ever be reunited.'

'You agreeing to come here is a start,' said Singh.

'To avoid giving you an excuse to attack,' said Lirra heatedly. 'We have no weapons.'

'Was that the only reason?'

'If you imprisoned me at least Haven would still have medicos to look after them.'

'I would have thought Micah Aristein would be keener to keep his young women close,' said Singh.

'I may choose not to breed!' retorted Lirra.

'Is that why Micah let you go?'

'Micah does not order; he discusses and advises. And we are not stupid! We remember what you did to us, could still do to us. I chose to come so you would not have any excuse to seize our medicos and force them to cure your ill by using the rest of us as hostages!'

She all but shouted the last bit and Seth and Dieter must have heard. Lirra rarely lost her temper and I was appalled she had now. It might have been tiredness or the stress of our situation but whatever the reason, she had just delivered Singh an awful lot of useful information.

'And you?' said Singh, turning to me. 'You give the impression you came here to fight or to exact revenge.' He paused. 'Or perhaps you already have,' he added softly.

Lirra stared at me too and for the first time since I had known her, there was fear in her eyes. She had just realised I had killed Seth's brother and the stakes had gone sky-high. I had never been a good liar and I was not about to try now. Singh might be a Mech but he reminded me of Micah, and Micah missed nothing.

I decided to tell the truth. 'I came because Lirra came,' I said. 'I am in love with her.'

12

My confession at least got us our own pod for the night, but it did not improve Lirra's temper. She stomped about the small space oblivious to the multitude of Human Well-being Systems surrounding us.

Holos; music from any of Earth's eras and sectors; treat food; health routines from yoga and meditation to combat; cleanliness cubicles that washed you with warm water you did not have to cart and dried you with pulses of perfumed air not rast towels that took off half your skin; and a latrine you did not have to turn with a hook-rake.

I worked my way through the music codes, pausing here and there to listen. Religious chants dedicated to a seventeenth century Christian god, mouth music from Mongolia—who knows what date, twentieth century pop from Britain, and Syntho Beat from the early thirtieth century.

I had just found something called Punk when Lirra snatched the code-bar from my hand and slammed it down on the table. 'We need to talk before you get us into even more trouble,' she hissed as she loomed over me.

'It was your idea to come here,' I said. 'I just tagged along after Adrian caught Imago-belly.'

'Iza-fungus belly you mean. Do not treat me like a fool, Warrain!'

'That is the last thing I would do,' I retorted, angry in turn. 'And as for me getting us into trouble, you would do well to think before revealing exactly how Micah runs Haven.'

'What do you mean?'

'Telling Singh Micah does not order people around, that once you had decided to come here, Micah would not try to stop you. Do you not think it would be useful to the Mechs to know Micah cannot make us fight? And that we have failed to get our hands on even a single weapon?'

'Singh would know that anyway from the Mechs that collected us. What he did not know was how to leverage us. Why did you spin him that crad about being in love with me?'

'I wanted to distract him from interrogating me over Seth's brother.' I reclaimed the code-bar and resumed my clicking as if my only concern were differentiating orchestral music from cappella.

Lirra sat down beside me. 'Did you kill him, Warrain?'

'Yes.'

'Is that how your face got scarred?'

'Yes.' Jazz filled my ears and I clicked onto what sounded like a funeral dirge, then Lirra's hand closed over mine and stilled the music, leaving the mournful strains to echo in my ears.

'Tell me what happened,' she said softly.

Her face was so tender I had to look away. 'I was in the tunnels and he fell through the roof in front of me. He reached for his weapon and I jumped him.'

'You shot him?'

'I strangled him.'

Lirra's revulsion was plain and it was my turn to stomp around the pod. 'SciCorp does not have the convenience of being able to kill from a distance,' I said bitterly.

'You dropped him down a shaft?'

'Where else?'

'Why did you not tell me, Warrain? We have never had secrets.'

'Oh, really? What about you and Adrian?'

'Do not be stupid!'

'Okay, then let us talk about the reason you sneaked away with SciCorp after the Fighting.'

'It is no secret I did not want to be part of the Mechs.'

'It is no secret either you chose to leave your mother behind unlike the rest of us who bawled our eyes out as we were dragged away. At the time, I thought it was because you were strong and the rest of us were weak, but after the way you cut your mother dead tonight, I am beginning to think there is more to it.'

Lirra held my gaze but it suddenly seemed I did not know her at all. Oh, I knew the curve of her brows, the liquid shine of her eyes, the full lips always ready to smile, but it was a child's understanding, like the way I had looked at Imago's opaque clouds but never really seen beyond them.

And then she dropped her head in a way that was almost submissive. 'You do not have to tell me,' I said hurriedly, dismayed by her reaction.

'My mother was having an affair with a Mech. I found out the evening of the Fighting.'

I trawled around for something to say but Lirra had not finished. 'I found out precisely the same time as my father. We had been on the beach and I had found a lis-nut just sprouting. I was so excited. I wanted to plant it at the Station, so I could have all the lis-juice I wanted. I wanted to show Pindan, so my father brought me back early.

'They were not exactly being discreet but the Mech was high on arrash. Maybe that is why he was careless or maybe it was his natural arrogance. You would have thought it was my father's right to be angry but apparently, it was the Mech's.

'I can still hear him screaming abuse, still see him raise his weapon, and then there was an explosion and I was wet.' Lirra's mouth twisted. 'It was why I cut my hair and stole new clothes. I was ashamed to wear my father's blood.'

'Lirra …' I wanted to hold her, but she half shook her head and wrapped her own arms about herself.

'You have not asked me the most important question, Warrain. You have not asked who the Mech was.'

There was something about the way she said it that turned my blood to ice. 'It was not Jacob, was it?'

'Got it in one. You never disappoint, Warrain. And how old is Pindan's eldest son?'

'Five,' I said hoarsely.

'Right again. My mother was pregnant by Jacob when we came home from the beach that afternoon and, even after he had murdered my father, she stayed with him to have another son.

'But that is not the worst of it, Warrain. It was my mother cheating with Jacob that started the Fighting. It was because of my mother you lost your family and SciCorp lost Station One.'

I do not recall exactly how we ended up in each other's arms in bed together but it was for comfort not sex. I was a virgin then and I suspect Lirra was too and neither of us in the mood for anything other than the warmth of each other's bodies. I set the code-bar so that Aboriginal music filled the pod but I do not know how authentic it was, only that, raw from the revelations of ugly truths, it was enough.

Memories of my ancestors are encoded in my DNA along with everything that marks me physically, and as I lay there in the sweet space I had carved out for my Dreaming, I could smell eucalyptus and feel the silk of red dust under my feet. I could even see the night sky: a deep black satin studded with dense milky swirls of stars.

It was the sky of ancestral creatures, some more human than others, and all intent on Creation. There were no Explorer Ships running on Earth's promise of power, no Settler Ships, and no Trads to disturb those other beings as they Dreamed their own worlds into existence, as my ancestors Dreamed my world into being, thousands of years before.

I do not know why thoughts of the maggot intruded at that moment. Imago was a long way from my ancestors and maggots a long way from the beauty of stars, but there she was in my mind's eye, as clear as if she were in the pod with us, her faceted eyes fixed on mine as her lipless mouth whispered my name.

We had already eaten when Fernandez came to the pod the next morning. I was glad it was not Seth or Dieter because if it were Fernandez's daughter in the Infirmary, he had more incentive to keep us alive. He brought a message from Singh that we were free until midday when he would meet with us again.

Lirra and I had no need to discuss where we would go; we wanted to see what state the beach was in. The third moon grew larger as it swung ever closer to Imago but the Mechs had no reason to stare skywards and even if they did, the arrival of a blanket of clouds made the moon hard to see unless you searched for it.

The moon's arrival was the most obvious change in Imago, but we still did not know whether it caused the sickness and if it did, how, and nor did we know whether the children had improved since our visit.

The Mechs had taken Lirra's advice and fed the children a broth thick with cress and olen-lichen harvested from beyond Station One's perimeter and it was a measure of their desperation they disregarded the data that showed the children's iron levels were normal. I tried not to think about the Mechs' retribution if the children worsened or died.

Our usual tag team of Seth and Dieter slouched along behind and I kept my voice low as we wound our way between the dunes. 'The lis-juice last night was not right,' I said.

'Mine tasted fine but it has been so long since I have had it, I cannot remember exactly what it should taste like,' said Lirra.

'It was not the taste that was off,' I said. 'It was something else.'

'Something else? Really Warrain, that is hardly scientific. Where is your proof?'

I knew Lirra was teasing. SciCorp insisted any conclusion to a problem must be supported by rigorously tested evidence, which was the exact opposite to how I operated.

My senses rarely let me down and when they had, it had simply been annoying. In contrast, being mistaken now could cost our lives. The realisation held me silent and Lirra took my hand.

'We are hardly walking like lovers,' she said, cosying up as we turned along the beach.

'That is because we are not.'

Her eyes flicked sideways. 'You really are out of sorts this morning. Anything I should know about?'

I wanted to tell her my confession of love had not been a subterfuge and that finally admitting my feelings had brought home to me just how precarious our situation was, but I said nothing. If Lirra believed we were just friends, she would be less likely to do something stupid to protect me and, as she had made no declaration of love, a friend was all I was.

'Warrain?'

Lirra was worried now and I brought her hand to my lips and kissed it. 'I am just trying to work out what is going on at Station One.'

'Let us ignore our IFNO tendencies and think logically,' said Lirra. 'Apart from anything else, it will please Petar and Thi that some of their endless instruction on the importance of objectivity has penetrated my thick IFNO skull.'

'So, what do we know?' I asked.

'There is a third moon obviously, but it might have been lurking out there for years. Without the 'scopes, it is hard to tell. And there are super high tides as you would expect with such a massive object drawing closer.'

I glanced at the debris strewn along the first line of dunes. 'We do not know how long the tides have been this high,' I pointed out, 'or whether our childhood memories of them are wrong.'

'True,' said Lirra, and grinned. 'You seem to be getting the hang of this scientific method thing quickly—for an IFNO.'

'And this lover thing,' I said, pulling her close and kissing her lightly on the lips.

'Oh, I think you were always a natural at that,' she said ambiguously. 'What else?'

My heart did an odd flip and I struggled to drag my attention back to the problem. 'If the high tides are due to the new moon, and if its gravitational pull is affecting Imago's soil, water, and flora, then it might result in sickness,' I said, 'especially if Station One's monitoring systems are also affected.

'Joseph reckons we have learned more about Imago's flora in the last five years than in all the time we spent at Station One because we have not had Station One's systems to rely on. Apparently, the threat of starvation is a marvellously motivating thing.'

'And then there are the maggots,' said Lirra, ignoring my quip, 'and whether they are a cause or an effect, or simply a coincidence.

'I do not follow.'

'Fernandez mentioned maggot sightings and you have seen some too,' said Lirra.

'I have seen one twice,' I corrected.

'Sergei reckons the covert plundering of the Protection Zone was so great it would have reduced the maggots to non-viable populations even before the Fighting, and the slaughter would have been worse after we were expelled.

'And yet they have been sighted again. So, the question is, whether their reappearance is linked to the third moon, or to the cause of the sickness, or to some other factor. They might even be responsible for the sickness. Then again, the timing of all these things could be a coincidence.'

'Our old friend coincidence is going to be hard to prove scientifically,' I ribbed.

'Or to disprove,' she retorted. 'Of course, we have not explored the most obvious reason for the children's illnesses and deaths.'

'Which is?'

'Station One. It was built as an autonomous functioning unit, almost organic in its design. Systems to regulate heat and cold, clothing and coverings, food and medicines, water purification and waste disposal. But what if the systems are breaking down?

'Not in a catastrophic way with balls of fire and black smoke, but more subtly, shifting out of alignment, purification not quite one hundred percent, data sheets ignoring aberrations they used to record. The anaemia was obvious in those children. They should not have needed a medico to diagnose it.'

'Maybe your diagnosis is wrong,' I forced myself to say. 'If we are using scientific method, we need to canvass that possibility as well.'

'Of course,' said Lirra tightly.

'Apart from anaemia, what else could cause their symptoms?'

'Blood loss, but they have suffered no wounds.'

'Could they be bleeding internally?'

'It is possible. I did not ask about their urine or faecal matter.' Lirra bit her lip and I could see she was upset with herself.

'The Mechs would have tested for it and Singh would have told us,' I reassured her. 'Is there any other reason why children would be affected apart from them being smaller?'

'It is not just body mass, Warrain. They are simply not as strong as adults.'

We came to a stop at a stand of palms splayed horizontally over the sand. Anders had once told me they were not palms at all but disk trees, but they were close enough to the palms that grew in Earth's tropics for homesick Settlers to call them such.

We rested our elbows on the trunks as we gazed out to sea. 'I am glad when I played here as a child, I did not know what was coming,' said Lirra.

'We still do not know what is coming.'

'You are right,' she said grudgingly, and turned so her back rested against the palm. 'I wish I knew how Mechs like them thought,' she said, her gaze on our guards.

'Oh, I can tell you that,' I said. 'We are the cause of all their problems, even the sickness indirectly. In expelling us, they took back what was rightfully theirs because they built Station One, but now they need us and nothing is guaranteed to deepen your hatred of an enemy more than needing them.'

Lirra looked troubled. 'They would prefer we failed?'

'Seth and Dietcr and their mates probably would but I doubt parents like Fernandez would, and certainly not Singh.'

'You are very astute, Warrain.'

I shrugged. 'None of this is scientific,' I pointed out.

'And neither is this,' she said, and brought her lips to mine. The kiss was long and sweet, and my blood surged like the seas to the moons' pull.

'I quite like this pretence of being lovers,' I said thickly, as she withdrew.

'I do not, but not for the reasons you think. Now back to the problem at hand. Let us assume Station One's systems are operating as normal but something has changed. How would we convince the Mechs to recalibrate the Station's systems?'

'Recalibrate?' I repeated, still grappling with Lirra's words. Did she mean she wanted our supposed relationship to be real, rather than pretence, or the prospect of sex with me was repellent?

'Reset their systems,' said Lirra impatiently.

'I know what recalibrate means, I just do not know if it is possible. I thought the systems were set on Earth, based on the data collected by the Explorer Ships.'

Space Corp's control of their galactic explorations had grown laxer over time and the data less reliable, but they still believed the best way to guarantee a Station's viability and to recoup their investment, was to make sure systems could not be tampered with by the unskilled.

There had been arguments over this even before our ship left Earth, for the very reasons that now confronted us. If a Sat changed, the systems could be rendered redundant, or worse, a danger to the very people they were supposed to protect.

According to Joseph, these objections were dismissed as uneconomic, although needless to say, that particular word was never used. Instead, Space Corp emphasised its commitment to safety in adhering to the most advanced technologies of off-planet habitation, and reiterated the dangers of allowing well-meaning, but alas, unskilled people to risk corrupting the systems on planets beyond the reach of immediate aid.

Lirra knew me well enough to wait for me to refocus before she continued. 'I do not think the Mechs have the expertise to recalibrate,' she said, 'but we might. I am guessing it would be more of a mathematical task than a technical one, but Micah would know.'

'We would have to convince the Mechs their systems were misaligned first and to allow Psycho Corp to interfere with them. And it might not be anything to do with the systems.'

'They have got dead and dying children the systems say are well!'

'Or who suffer from something too subtle for the systems to pick up,' I countered.

'True,' said Lirra, 'and we are no closer to finding out what it is.'

13

In the silence that followed, I became aware of the slide and suck of the waves and of the papery rustle of fronds above. The air was full of salt and I breathed it deep into my lungs, wishing the shore was mine again and I was free to enjoy it with Lirra.

But wishes were for children and we had armed Mechs less than thirty lengths away and a problem that if we failed to solve, could cost us Haven.

'I vote for giving up on scientific method,' I said, with forced lightness.

'Not yet. We have not considered the third moon or the maggots.'

'Let us start with the moon,' I said, reluctant to reveal the details of my last encounter with the maggot.

'The planet formerly known as XF-2010BX1 and now officially designated Imago, has two moons,' began Lirra in a monotone. 'One is five times the size of the other, but both have a similar mass to the Earth's moon.

'Earth's moon revolves once on its axis, thus presenting the same face to Earth. It completes a revolution of the Earth once every twenty-nine and a half Earth days. Imago's moons behave in a similar manner. Named after gods of the Ancients, each moon turns once on its axis and so presents the same face to Imago. Each moon completes a revolution of Imago in thirty-one Imagoan days.

'The moons' orbits are so close to each other that, in terms of gravitational pull, they act as a single body. Thus, the oceans abutting Station One and the adjacent bays, experience similar tidal frequencies to those on Earth. Imago's axial tilt results in four temperate seasons and the tidal ranges vary as a result.'

'You sound like a data-slab,' I said, impressed.

'So I should. I spent a lot of time reading on the way out and it did not take me long to get through the so-called children's library. And Joseph is always keen to tell his stories.'

'So, you know a lot about everything,' I said.

'I know a lot about the little Space Corp bothered to supply us with. Storing the rest in the Data Pod was a mistake.'

'But cost effective,' I said sourly. 'I wonder if the Data Pod could tell us what we want to know anyway.'

'Whether a third moon was recorded by the Explorer Ships? The size and shape of its orbit? The moon's mass and gravitational pull? Its effects on the oceans?'

'And whether it inflicts some sort of illness,' I added.

'Its gravitational pull might be small but still big enough to alter the chemical composition of plants,' said Lirra thoughtfully.

'Given the tides, it does not look small.'

'The arrival of a third moon, high tides, sick and dying children, and the reappearance of maggots. Tell me what you know of the maggots, Warrain.'

'You go first,' I said, still wanting to delay the uncomfortable conversation. 'You have probably read all there is on the subject on the way here and put up with Joseph's ramblings since.'

'The Explorer Ships recorded them as the most intelligent of the life-forms they surveyed, but that is not saying much. They were six on the ILFII.'

I was familiar with most of the acronyms Space Corp used and knew that ILFII stood for Indigenous Life-Forms Intelligence Index. But six meant nothing to me.

'How intelligent is six?' I asked.

'Not very. The scale goes up to ten. The Explorer Ships noted signs of self-awareness, social organisation, and primitive communication. They saw no sign of pair-bonds between adults, or between adults and juveniles.'

'Knowing the Explorer Ships, I doubt they looked very hard,' I said. People who signed up to spend years in the dark holes of deep space were not attracted by scientific record-keeping but by coin, adventure, and the opportunity to rip valuables from Sats before Space Corp imposed some sort of order.

'They did note some physical details,' said Lirra. 'The maggots were up to two metres in length, limbless, with leathery bodies and with locomotion that resembled a caterpillar. The most common colour was greyish white.'

'Hence the name maggot,' I said.

'Yes,' said Lirra. 'The tissue samples they retrieved identified them as the pupae of some sort of insect, which is why they named

81

the planet Imago. It is the final adult stage of an insect,' she added, in response to my blank look.

'Oh, I thought it must be the name of some Commander's mistress,' I quipped. Lirra rolled her eyes and I sobered. 'Given the place was full of maggots and not flies, why not call the planet Maggot or Grub?'

'For the same reason the Ancients called a lump of frozen rock Greenland.'

'What?'

Lirra sighed. 'They needed to attract Settlers to protect and extract the DEMs. People are hardly likely to queue up to spend the rest of their lives on a Sat which has connotations of flyblown meat.'

'But the maggots do not look like maggots or grubs now,' I said, my mind full of the silvery human-like creature I had seen.

'No. Even when we first established Station One, they did not look like maggots. Joseph has kept the best records of anyone and he says there has been no known sightings of anything resembling what the Explorer Ships reported and, because it is unethical to take tissue samples from previously classified species, we do not know exactly how they have changed.'

'But we have theories about why they changed,' I said, grimacing as I visualised men from the Explorer Ships creating the present maggot-human hybrids. Some members of SciCorp argued this next generation of humanoid maggots were the final imago stage and the Explorer Ships had nothing to do with the changes, but the maggots' human characteristics were too strong to convince most of the scientists.

In any case, the time-frame was all wrong. Since the establishment of Station One, there had been no sightings of juvenile maggots and that supported the theory the hybrids were sterile adults.

If that were the case, the hermaphrodite form of the maggot had been stopped dead by the intrusion of the Explorer Ships, a catastrophe that condemned the maggots to extinction. It would not be the first species destroyed by the arrival of the Explorer Ships or by Settlers.

'So,' continued Lirra, 'after we were expelled from Station One, the Mechs wiped out the last of the maggots from the Protection Zone they had secretly hunted from the start. And according to Fernandez, no more maggots were seen at Station One until recently, and Haven has had no sightings at all, apart from yours, that is. Over to you, Warrain.'

'Both times the maggot was in a tunnel south of Haven,' I said slowly.

'Are you sure they were not different maggots? The Explorer Ships recorded maggots as being undifferentiated and sightings of the hybrid form since say the same.'

'It was the same one. The first time she took off but the second time she stayed.'

'She?'

'Definitely she,' I said.

Lirra sifted her breath through her teeth. 'Okay. But if anyone else but you claimed a maggot-hybrid was female, I would argue. Given she hung around the second time, you must have had a good look at her.'

I nodded and gave a brief description.

'Why do you think she did not run the second time?' asked Lirra. 'Was she curious?' I said nothing and Lirra's eyes narrowed. 'What is it you have not told me, Warrain?'

'The maggot said my name.'

Lirra's draw dropped. 'The maggot said your name?'

'Yes. I saw her mouth move and she said my name. It was soft and a little slurred, but it was my name, not some hiss or gurgle, and not the sound of the wind in the striate, or an echo off the valley's side.'

'Why did you not tell me this earlier?'

'I never really got the chance, plus …' I traced the roughness of the palm's bark with my fingers. Lirra waited and I glanced back to her. 'It was unnerving. The maggot looked at me like you are looking at me now, and then she said my name.'

'Did she say anything else?'

'No, because at that moment, you arrived and the maggot took off like she had the first time.'

'A moon appears, and maggots are seen again, and one of them, a female, calls you by name. The odds are shortening these things are linked.'

'The odds are shortening it is magic,' I said dourly.

'And if this one is female, it means they are still capable of shifting between male and female, which hybridisation was thought to stop,' continued Lirra thoughtfully, ignoring my comment.

'None of it explains how she knew my name or how to say it.'

'I like your suggestion of magic,' said Lirra, with a grin.

'So do I, if it works against the Mechs.' I glanced back along the beach. 'Looks like time is up.'

Seth and Dieter headed in our direction and not for the first time I wished I had taken the weapon off Seth's brother. I might have had the chance to steal ammunition here, but I had not known I would be here then.

'We have explored lots of interesting things,' said Lirra, sounding disturbingly like Joseph.

'But found no answers.'

'Yet,' she said determinedly.

We held our silence as we made our way back to Station One, but Seth and Dieter did not take us to Singh's rooms but to the Infirmary. A grim-looking Fernandez waited for us and Seth and Dieter took up positions behind us, in front of the closed door, weapons in hands. Singh's absence was also a bad sign.

'Your medicines are not doing the good you intended,' said Fernandez. 'If good is what you intended.'

I edged closer to Lirra as I swiftly calculated where we could shelter if the weapons started blasting, but Lirra's head came up. 'I came here to cure not to kill! Are you saying they are worse?'

'They are no better.'

'Are you giving them the broth?' she demanded.

'Of course!'

'And checking your system's data?'

'That is not your concern.'

'It is when it is wrong. What changes does it show?'

'No changes at all, as expected. The children remain gravely ill.'

'No changes at all, as expected,' mimicked Lirra. 'Think about it, Fernandez. The broth I prescribed is dense in iron. The systems should have picked up the chemical changes in their bodies.'

Fernandez's jaw set and Lirra angrily rammed home her point. 'You have sick and dying children and systems that say nothing is wrong. I am not pretending to know the cause of their illness, Fernandez, but it is my job to search for it. Your job, if you are willing to take it on, is to work out why your systems have failed.'

That ended the discussion, but Seth and Dieter were just as frustrated as Fernandez, and their weapons jabbed us in the back as they marched us to Singh's pod. Seth itched for an excuse to dish out violence, but I was not about to risk Lirra by providing him with one. I just hoped she was not either. Her anger was palpable.

Nothing about our detour to the Infirmary was good news. I was pretty sure Singh's orders were to bring us straight to him and the Mechs' behaviour told me Singh's control of the Station was weak. It was unsurprising given Mechs equated manliness with physical strength.

While Seth and Dieter's feelings for us reflected mine for them, Fernandez seemed willing to listen and I do not think it was only because one of the sick children was probably his.

His rationality was one of the few positives of our predicament that and he ranked higher than Seth and Dieter. I guessed he would have the Mechs check and re-check the systems until they located the malfunction. I hoped it would take them a long time, not because I wished their children harm, but because it gave Seth less time to plan my murder.

Singh was seated in his usual chair when we entered but his eyes were ringed with black and his skin sallow against the red swirl of material on his head.

'I believe you have been to the Infirmary,' he said, and I nodded. 'My reports tell me the children are no worse but as Tom Fernandez's daughter is amongst the ill, he is keen to see quicker progress. On the other hand, Seth McKenzie and Dieter Schumann are simply keen for an excuse to kill you.'

I blinked and Singh smiled wearily. 'I am aware of most things that happen at Station One,' he said.

'That may be so,' retorted Lirra. 'But Fernandez and Co's actions tell me you are not really in charge of them.'

I flinched at her bluntness but Singh seemed unperturbed. 'Most likely you are right,' he said. 'I suppose you wonder why I tolerate such insubordination?'

'Yes, I do.'

'I presume you are familiar with the Space Corp policy of replicating Earth-based societies in their Settler Programs?'

'They select from different races, religions and genders,' I said quickly. I had no idea where Singh was headed with this, but I wanted to get in before Lirra said something even more inflammatory.

'In the hope of creating the same harmonious history Earth is famous for,' said Singh ironically. 'Given the dealings between the Mechtechnicians and SciCorp, I suppose they have succeeded.

'Even so, Space Corp's notion of representativeness has varied over time. I can only assume the moderates were in charge when they drew up the Settler list for Imago. Not only did they look beyond the usual religious affiliations of the big three: Judaism, Islam and Christianity, but they included Taoists, Buddhists and Sikhs, and even a few IFNO's.'

Singh's gentle humour did nothing to pacify Lirra. 'They really were radical,' she sneered.

'And perhaps prescient,' said Singh, unruffled by Lirra's jibe. 'Amongst the Mechtechnicians, we have some whose religions are less inclined to violence than others. Some of these took part in the Fighting, high on arrash and misplaced loyalty, but once the arrash disappeared, they remembered the more peaceful teachings of their gods.'

'Their gods did not stop them from murdering,' said Lirra.

'No. but their gods have made them reluctant to do so again and encouraged them to appoint me their Commander, despite the weaponry lodged in my back and my stated intention to seek reunification with SciCorp.'

For a moment, I thought I had misheard him and, in the silence that followed, I could almost hear Lirra's brain ticking over. I resisted the urge to yell that I wanted nothing to do with the stinking Mechs, now or ever, but things were not nearly as clear cut for Lirra. Her passion lay in healing and there was a lot of very useful medical equipment lying idle at Station One.

'Whatever the situation is now,' continued Singh, 'Space Corp's first forays into the galaxy were underpinned by the noblest of intentions, namely, to establish harmonious settlements and nurture and protect life in all its manifestations.

'And yet so many of the Sats have been plagued by squabbles and the destruction of their indigenous life-forms. We have replicated the worst of what we left behind on Earth but there is still a chance to create something better.'

'What religion are you?' asked Lirra abruptly.

'Sikh,' said Singh.

Lirra had read even the most boring of the data-slabs on the long voyage from Earth and kept company with Joseph since, but she looked as lost as I was.

'Religious beliefs are not a predictor of how people behave,' said Singh, 'and as we know, Earth's histories are littered with atrocities committed in the name of this or that god.

' Suffice to say I am not alone in wanting Station One to be as it was intended: Mechtechnicians and SciCorp working together for the common good.'

Singh's sentiments were genuine but what the crad did it mean for us and for Mechs like Seth and Dieter?

'Is that what all the Mechs want?' I asked.

'Many are content with the way things are,' admitted Singh, 'and the younger Mechtechnicians have no experience of the excitement of exploring the complexities of Imago's fauna and flora. They do not perceive the link between the Mechtechnicians' role in building Station One and SciCorp's role in using it to carry out Space Corp work. It is a lack that must be rectified.'

He shifted in his seat and grimaced. 'What of Station Two?' he asked. 'Is there talk of a return to Station One at some time in the future? Of reunification?'

'SciCorp has no need of the Mechs,' I said.

'But you have need of our systems,' said Singh. 'Everything you need to observe the stars, to analyse blood and tissue samples, to test sap and soil, everything remains in Station One.'

'We have developed our own methods,' I retorted.

'I have no doubt you have. I have never underestimated the intelligence and ingenuity of SciCorp but no matter how cleverly you have sought to replicate the equipment of Station One, I am certain you have failed.

'Imago does not have the polymers, metals, or synths to manufacture what the Settler Ships brought in the pods. While you remain isolated in Station Two, you will never be able to accomplish the work that was your reason for coming here.'

Singh was probably right but I was so incensed I did not trust myself to speak. Having forced us out from Station One five years ago, Singh now tried to force us back in. His methods were not as crude this time around, but they might be just as effective.

I had seen Petar, Thi, Sing and Sergei and countless others of SciCorp look towards Sapphire Bay and curse, not just the Mechs, but the loss of their instruments and data-slabs.

'You are right, of course,' said Lirra, her voice thick with emotion. 'What we need to do our jobs, in the way Earth envisioned, is here. But maybe the way Earth envisioned things is no longer relevant.

'Maybe Earth itself is no longer relevant. Earth has forgotten us or else turned inward, intent now on its own affairs. We can no longer rely on it like a child relies on its mother.

Five years ago, the men you now lead murdered us, tore children from their mother's arms, and drove us out.

'But I do not think these things are the only reason we will never reunite. It is what followed that bloody day. You gave us a pretty stark choice: claw out another home for ourselves or die. We survived but we are no longer Station One exiles or even SciCorp, desperate to get our hands back on our instruments and to return to our old ways of doing. We are something else now. Not Imagoan exactly, but no longer just Settlers.

'Yet here nothing has changed. You still live behind a voltaged fence, eat the food the systems provide, believe in their infallibility, even when . . .' Lirra's voice cracked and she took a shuddering breath, 'even when your children die and the systems say they are well.'

There was a short silence. 'Is that what Micah Aristein believes too?' asked Singh heavily. The lines had deepened around his mouth and he looked drained.

'We do not know what Micah believes,' I admitted, taking Lirra's hand. 'Maybe a couple of years ago, SciCorp would have leapt at the opportunity to return home, as we used to call Station One, but I do not hear anyone call it home anymore or waste time discussing it.

'As you have pointed out, SciCorp does not have the benefit of what was unloaded from the Settler Ships. We work hard to put food in our bowls, to stay warm in winter, to keep our children safe and healthy.'

Singh wiped his face wearily. 'We have more in common than you think,' he said slowly. 'Tomorrow I will see whether your broths have served our children well and whether our systems have too. Then I will arrange your return to Station Two. I have a message that needs to be delivered to Micah Aristein, and too much time has elapsed to delay any longer.'

We took our midday meal in our pod, mainly to avoid the gaze of others, but it was no hardship given the novelty of the food systems that delivered exotic treats by punching in a code. Lirra prowled around the small space while I lounged on the bed nibbling on this and that while I watched her.

'I liked your speech about us being different,' I said. 'It really set Singh back on his heels.'

'I did not say it for effect,' she growled. 'None of this is a game.'

'I never said it was, not when they have weapons.'

'And it is not about your craddy weapons!' she said, rounding on me. 'It is about building something new and if Micah agrees to reunite, we will be back to something old and decaying and rotten.'

'I do not think Micah wants to come back and I bet the majority of Mechs do not want us back either, not if Seth and his mate are anything to go by. If the Mechs can sort out their systems, they will not need us anyway and we certainly do not need them.'

Lirra stopped her pacing but she hugged herself and again I resisted the urge to let my arms replace hers. There was no reason in private to pretend we were lovers.

'You realise if any SciCorp want to return to Station One, Micah will let them go,' said Lirra. 'And if enough of them leave, Haven will not be viable. We will be reduced to scratching out a living like the maggots.'

I scowled as the vision of the maggot invaded my head. What was it about her that so disturbed me? Her silvery, faceted eyes? Her sibilant voice saying my name? These things did not make her human, I reminded myself, and for all Lirra's yearning to be Imagoan, I wondered if the closest we would get were glimpses of a species we had already destroyed.

15

I would have lazed away the day reacquainting myself with all the tech-bits Station One had on offer but Lirra thought revisiting the gardens was a better use of my time than playing with Station One's toys.

I did not think watching the holos those on Earth used for entertainment was a waste of time, especially those on weapon usage, but there was no way I was letting Lirra go anywhere alone.

As we made our way across the synth-turf, I tried to match my childhood memories with my surroundings. I wanted to locate the weapons' store but did not have much luck. The Mechs probably stashed their weapons somewhere else by now anyway and, even if they did not, my chances of breaking into it and getting out of the Station alive, were non-existent. Even so, the possibility of stealing Mech weapons was tempting.

The gardens were deserted but Lirra made her way up and down the rows of vegetables as methodically as she had on day one. I trailed behind, my head full of visions of blasting away with weapons as the Mechs ran for their lives.

'Come back to me, Warrain,' she snapped, 'and use those black fella senses to tell me what is wrong, not plot revenge.'

I did not bother arguing; we both knew she was right. I took a lungful of air and, as I exhaled, tried to let my anger and resentment go too. I became aware of the cool breeze on my skin, of the slight chemical smell of the synth-turf, of the sound of the sea in the distance, and of the taint of rottenness.

I had smelled it before and while it was stronger now, it was no easier to identify. I crouched beside a row of something that had been harvested, pulled out a ragged stalk and brought it to my nose.

The smell was weaker than expected and I put my face close to the hole and inhaled. That turned out to be a mistake. The wave of nausea was so strong I all but fell sideways.

Lirra grabbed my arm. 'What is it?' she hissed.

'The ground is putrid.'

'You mean the synth-turf?'

'I mean the ground.' I hauled myself upright and sucked in air while Lirra grappled with what I had said. The smell remained in my nostrils, sourer than vomit. 'I am going to the shore,' I muttered, needing its fresh winds.

Lirra kept pace but I was scarcely aware of her or of the Mechs who trailed in our wake, beyond noted they were not Seth and Dieter. But the shore was not the cure-all I hoped for, and it certainly was not a comfort. If there had been a storm during the night we would have heard it, but the night had been calm, unlike the ocean.

The palms we had leaned on the previous day had been wrenched out and washed up the beach. I glanced back at the Mechs, half expecting one of them to rush off to Station One to report the damage, but while they looked about curiously, nothing suggested any upset or urgency.

Lirra stretched, pretending to luxuriate in the salty air, and took a long hard look at the sky.

'We have got problems,' she murmured.

I picked up a pebble and threw back my head as I skimmed it into the waves. Little of the sky was visible, thanks to the heavy cloud, but I knew where to look. 'Station One certainly has,' I said. The third moon was enormous.

Our escorts were bent over something and my heart quickened before I realised it was one of their tech-bit games. Lirra's claim the safe and predictable life of Station One had diminished rather than grown the Mechs rang true. They were lesser now than when they had arrived, for then they had had the demanding job of a Station to build.

'If Station One goes under, the Mechs will take Haven,' said Lirra.

Cold dread tightened my guts. I would have my revenge but so too would the Mechs. I was glad Joseph was not around to point out the irony. 'Another tide like the last will breach the dunes,' I said slowly. 'Then it is about two hundred lengths to the fence.'

'Of gentle slope. If there is an onshore wind, it could do it tonight.'

'Unless the moon swings away again.'

'Unless God intervenes,' said Lirra tightly.

'Which one?' I joked, despite feeling anything but light-hearted.

'Take your pick.'

'It would help Micah and Ivan to calculate the new moon's orbit if they had access to a 'scope,' I said.

Lirra's eyes flashed to mine. 'It will not help anyone if you are dead, Warrain, and do not even think about raiding their weapons store!'

'It would even things up if they came for Haven.'

'You want to be a murderer too, Warrain?'

'I already am.'

In that moment, the full gravity of what I had done finally sank in. My boyhood dream of defeating the Mechs to honour my father and take back Station One, was just that: the dream of an embittered boy who had seen his father killed and been wrenched from his mother.

It had sustained me into adulthood but for the first time, I saw what it had cost me. Lirra trained to nourish life, not to take it, and the boys who had trudged away with me from Station One with grubby, tear-stained faces, acquired the skills Haven needed to thrive.

All I could claim were the skills of a killer, and not a very good one at that. I had simply been luckier than the Mech and I wondered if I would be lucky next time or whether I could bear the horror of killing again.

'You did not have any choice, Warrain.'

'No,' I said, keeping my gaze on the sea. It was grey, reflecting the scud of clouds above; Station One was in for rain.

'If you had gone out and not come back, you would have killed part of me too.'

I stared at her in confusion. 'Killed part of you?'

Lirra's mouth kinked into a smile. 'Yes. Guess which part?' I had trouble meeting her eyes and looked back to the sea. 'We need to get back,' she said abruptly. 'We need to tell Singh what we have found.'

She strode off, a sure sign she was annoyed with me, and I knew why. She had given me the perfect opportunity to declare my feelings for her and I had failed the test, my head too full of my other failures.

I hurried after her. 'I do not think we should tell Singh about the moon,' I said.

'Singh wants peace and he wants reunification,' she flung over her shoulder. 'He has a right to know.'

'That is what he says but he could be playing political games.'

'If you believe that Warrain, I have been totally wrong about you all these years and you have absolutely no ability to sense the truth in anything.'

'It is Micah's decision whether we tell the Mechs,' I said. The argument was weak and we both knew it.

'Micah sent us here to heal Station One's children, not to let them die,' she shot back.

'We will tell Singh about the ground then; that they will need to harvest their food from beyond Station One until they work out what is wrong under the synth-turf, or until their systems do. We do not tell him anything else.'

Lirra slewed to a stop. 'So, when Singh asks whether we have any idea what caused the problem, we are going to say no when it is pretty obvious it is the third moon?'

'We do not know that. Just because two things happen together does not mean one causes the other. You should know that, Lirra, giving your medico training.' The last comment was supposed to defuse the situation but it had the opposite effect.

'Believe me, Warrain, if I were to give into the urge to punch you, it would certainly be caused by what you just said!'

The rest of the journey was undertaken in stony silence but Station One was anything but quiet. Mechs milled about the yard and Fernandez was positioned at the gate as if he waited for our return.

'Looks like they might know,' I whispered, as we drew near.

Fernandez came forward to meet us, several weapons stuck in his belt. 'Commander Singh wants to see you immediately,' he said.

We did not risk speaking again but I caught Lirra's hand and our fingers meshed. Angry shouts came from beyond one of the pods as we were hustled across the yard and, while I did not catch the words, I guessed they were not wishing us good health.

There were armed Mechs outside Singh's pod and I wondered whether they were there to escort us to our place of execution. Fernandez knocked once and ushered us in then took up position inside the room facing the door, which meant his back was to us. Lirra shot me a questioning look but I had no idea what it meant either.

Singh had looked tired last time we met but now he looked positively exhausted. 'Do you have anything further to report?' he asked.

'Something has altered in the soil beneath the synth-turf in your gardens,' I said quickly, before Lirra could speak. 'I sensed it yesterday but today it is unmistakable. It is probably affecting your crops but maybe not enough for your systems to pick up.'

'But enough for your children to sicken,' broke in Lirra. 'You need to stop using the gardens until you ascertain the cause. The broths are from cresses harvested beyond the fence and should not be affected.' She paused. 'Have the children improved?'

'Yes, according to their carers. The systems show no change.'

'But they did not show the children were ill in the first place,' I pointed out.

'Precisely,' said Singh.

He stared down at the desk as if he contemplated how to break some extremely bad news and I snatched a glance at Lirra. Her chin was up as if she already braved the death-march through the jeering crowd outside. In contrast, my brain frenetically clicked through the possibilities of snatching Fernandez's weapons and shooting our way out or taking Singh hostage.

Singh picked up a message pouch and turned it over in his hands. No doubt it contained the death warrant, with his and probably Cohen's signatures on it to ensure all was in order should the IJ ships return. If I were going to jump Fernandez, it had to be now.

'I have a message here for Commander Micah Aristein,' said Singh, holding it out to me. My astonishment must have been obvious and for a moment I made no move to take it. 'It formally outlines my request for a peaceful reunification and invites discussions. It also extends my personal best wishes.'

I took the pouch and thrust it deep into my pocket, too stunned to speak.

'What is going on outside?' asked Lirra, her usual bluntness unaffected.

'We have had an increase in maggot sightings recently,' said Singh. 'Last night their numbers increased dramatically, almost as if they have swarmed. They streamed past the perimeter fence in the direction of the Iron Ranges. Apart from the extraordinary sight they presented, they brought with them the scent of arrash.'

The room stilled. 'How many addicts do you have?' asked Lirra.

'What …' I began before understanding dawned. 'But surely after all this time …'

'Time makes no difference, Warrain,' said Lirra. 'Addiction re-wires the brain permanently.'

'There are fourteen addicts from the time of the Fighting,' said Singh, 'including Jacob. But most were functioning until last night.'

'And now?'

'Twelve have relapsed and another ten had their first taste.'

Twenty-two! My blood ran cold at the threat these men posed and then horror overwhelmed me as I thought of the maggots' slaughter.

Had the female maggot been butchered too? Her body drained of the essence addicts found irresistible? The uneasy excitement of the Mechs outside made sense now, as did the shouts from the holding pods. Fernandez did not guard the door against our escape but against intruders! And it was not our skins in danger but Singh's!

'How risky is it for you?' I asked.

'That depends on how many more Mechtechnicians decide the fantasy world of arrash is superior to the real one of Imago. The odds are presently in my favour but that could change. It is best you start your journey back to Station Two now. If the maggots resume their migration tonight, it would be safest if you were long gone.'

'I will ensure Micah receives your message,' I said, with an awkward bow.

I did not look at Lirra as I headed for the door, simply willed her to follow and she did. Fernandez escorted us back to the pod where we reclaimed our packs, and then to the gate.

'Thank you for your aid,' he said, and closed the gate behind us.

We made the first part of the journey in silence, saving our breath for our speedy climb. It would have been easier to travel along the side of the valley but I led the way straight up the spur. I wanted to be clear of Station One and its arrash-addled Mechs as fast as possible and I wanted to be able to see if anyone followed.

The stiff breeze grew to a gusty wind but Lirra and I did not don our jackets until we reached the top and the rain started. The sinking sun fired the clouds emerald and magenta but there was no time to admire them as we pushed on through the rain until we reached a cave I had discovered on a previous ramble.

'Do you want to stop here or keep going?' I asked.

'Why bother asking what I want?'

It was hard to see her face, for the dark had closed in, but her tone was clear enough. Lirra was not the type to sulk or stew and I waited.

'It was dishonest not to warn Singh about the tides,' she said, 'especially as he is under threat.'

'That is precisely why we could not warn him,' I said.

'Oh really? How could helping him possibly be a problem?'

'If we told Singh Station One was likely to flood in the next few nights, what do you think he would do?'

'Order an evacuation.'

'To where?'

There was a long pause. 'Haven,' she said in a small voice. 'But we could accommodate them, Warrain, if Station One were uninhabitable. Micah would agree and it is what Singh wants too, in a roundabout way.'

'Singh wants us to return to Station One, but I am sure if Station One were wiped out, he would live with us peaceably at Haven.'

Lirra looked at me in confusion. 'So why not warn him?'

'Because chances are, we will not be dealing with Singh. Chances are, Lirra, Singh will not be leader but some arrash-addled thug and there will be no peaceable joining, just another murderous takeover.'

'But what is to stop them doing that anyway?'

'Us and our start on them. If the Mechs knew they were to be inundated, they would not have let us go. They are not going to claw out another Station when there is a perfectly good one for the taking.'

'So, we get back and warn Micah. Then what?'

'I do not know but at least we will not be taken by surprise like last time. And we know the Ranges and the shafts, and we are not totally defenceless.'

Lirra snorted. 'Matra knives against weaponry? Not very equal, is it?'

'More equal than last time,' I said stubbornly.

At least Lirra was convinced enough by the scenario to push on through the night and that suited me. Despite the rain and heavy cloud, once the moons rose, there was enough light to travel safely. The brightness told me the third moon must be even bigger and my heart went out to Singh.

I knew Lirra thought me callous or ruthless or both, and she was probably right. I hoped the Mechs loyal to Singh would protect him, but I was not convinced they could, not when a fresh supply of arrash trooped past their front door. But of one thing I was certain: if it came to a choice between Singh's welfare and Haven's, Haven won, hands down.

It was close to midnight when we heard the first shot. We stopped and stared back towards Station One as if we could pierce the gloom and distance to see what happened there. More shots rang out and then a volley that lasted for more than a minute, and then there was silence.

'Are they shooting each other or the maggots?' asked Lirra, instinctively whispering.

'Each other, I hope,' I said, then realised I did not hope that at all. Singh was there, and Lirra's mother and brothers, and the sick children.

I did not even wish Fernandez harm because he loved his daughter and I had just discovered what love meant. If I hoped anything at all it was the addicts wiped each other out. I detested them slaughtering the maggots to feed their greed but I also yearned to be free of their threat.

But there was another fear I could barely admit even to myself: that the third moon heralded the final phase of SciCorp's destruction begun five years earlier. And as I watched Lirra hug herself in some vain search for comfort, I resolved anything the Mechs' stole from us this time, would cost them as much in blood as it cost us.

I reached for her hand. 'Let us go,' I said, but then something moved in the darkness. I threw myself in front of her and frantically searched for some sort of weapon. The best I could find was a stone but Lirra's hand fastened on my wrist before I could hurl it.

'It is a maggot,' she whispered.

She was right but I was so rattled I was not convinced the maggot was not dangerous too. Its silvery eyes glimmered as it turned its head towards us but it continued up the slope at the same unhurried pace and disappeared into the darkness.

'W-was that the one you saw before?' asked Lirra.

I shook my head, overcome with relief it was not Seth. If any Mech came after us, I sensed it would be him. We went on, seeing another half dozen or so maggots before the clouds' purplish blush told us the night was over.

The other maggots moved at the same slow pace but the female I had seen had been fast and I wondered whether speed varied with sex. Being slow was hardly an advantage for males though; not with the Mechs picking them off.

The new day was just as wet but I was glad because the clouds hid the third moon and that bought us time, the one thing that could save us. It was midmorning before we stopped under a shallow overhang.

We ate the zitin cakes we had taken with us from Haven, coated with chillie-lichen, I collected as we had walked. The lichen delivered a comforting warmth that Lirra warned not to confuse with sustenance.

The food also delivered a wave of drowsiness and I saw Lirra yawn. 'Do you want a quick sleep?' I asked. 'I will keep watch.'

'You need sleep as much as I do and we both know we do not have time.'

'If we can keep going through the day, we can snatch some sleep tonight,' I said. 'We will be less than a day from Haven then.'

'We will rest at midday,' said Lirra. 'Sleep deprivation is akin to arrash and that will not help our chances of beating the Mechs to Haven.'

I made no reply. Lirra had an unhappy knack of putting my fears into words and that left nothing more to say.

16

I considered the effects of arrash as we walked, searching for something that might help us in any fighting to come. Arrash was highly addictive and, like most alpha opioids, users needed more and more to get the same effect. In the end, they were so desperate for it they allowed nothing to stand in their way: not love or loyalty or consequences.

Given that, my guess was Singh and his supporters were already dead. Which meant? Celebrations at Station One? Mechs high on arrash killing maggots for fun? Killing each other? And if the sea had surged over the last row of dunes, had they noticed? And if so, were they hot on our heels, intent on setting up home at Haven? And if so, how the crad were we to stop them?

'What is worrying you, Warrain?' I looked at Lirra blankly. 'You have not spoken for hours. Let me in,' she added softly.

'What is there not to worry about?' I asked, with a poor attempt at humour. Lirra's honey eyes tugged at my depths as they always had and I took a deep breath. 'I am trying to think of a weapon we have that the Mechs do not,' I admitted.

'Oh, you should have asked me sooner and saved yourself some stress,' said Lirra. 'There is not one.'

'Thanks,' I said, and stomped on, but Lirra's arm looped through mine so her body pressed against my side. Her warmth and familiar scent comforted me but also reminded me of how much I had to lose.

I had an urge to take her in my arms and tell her how much I loved her, but I resisted the impulse. At the time I thought the attack of sentimentality was brought on by tiredness and it was only later I realised what a fool I was not to have said those words. Instead I racked my brains for something that could defeat the Mech's weapons.

'A better question might be what the Mechs have that we do not,' said Lirra, after a while.

'Same thing,' I said irritably. 'And the answer is everything.'

'It is not the same thing. We saw at Station One how having everything can work against you.'

'You mean the Mechs believing their systems saying everything was okay when it clearly was not?' I said.

'Yes, and their lack of interest in what happened around them. You would think they would keep an eye on the ocean for one thing. Apart from being right on their doorstep, it could tell them a lot about what is normal on Imago and what is not.'

'And their susceptibility to arrash. It must be a Mech weakness.'

'Addiction is not linked to occupation,' said Lirra.

My head swivelled. 'Are you saying there are arrash users amongst SciCorp?'

'Were arrash users.'

'So,' I said, as my tired brain slogged through the implications, 'if the maggots come anywhere near Haven, we could find ourselves in the same deep crad as Station One.'

'Use your considerable intelligence, Warrain. Do you think Micah would have left our addicts untreated? And as you keep pointing out, we do not have weapons. If SciCorp addicts want to kill and milk maggots, they have to do so with matra knives.'

'It is still possible,' I persisted.

'Anything is possible,' said Lirra, 'even you admitting you are wrong.'

We stopped again at midday and by then Lirra and I had ceased speaking; the result of exhaustion, not any argument. The drizzle persisted and when a stiff breeze joined it, we left the exposed stone of the spur and came down into the valley.

Apart from the wind and rain, we had good reason to leave the ridge top. The view of Sapphire Bay I had hoped for was blocked by clouds but there was enough light to make us visible against the sky.

We did not descend to the valley floor but followed one of the paths along the valley's side. SciCorp still debated whether these were really paths or some sort of geological formation.

They ran in parallel lines along the valleys' walls and some SciCorp speculated they were migratory tracks worn by generations of some now extinct species. Others argued the ridges were so regular in the seaward-facing valleys they had to be the edges of rock strata.

I was not thinking of any of these theories as I made my way along one; simply glad to be out of the wind and keen to find somewhere snug to rest. The path was wide enough to walk side by side but Lirra followed as the rain made the stone slick and neither of us trusted the edges.

We did not descend into the striate until the last of the light waned. The gloomy weather meant it was even darker there but it was dry amongst the detritus. We carved out a bit of a nest hard up against a trunk out of the rain, ate and curled up together for warmth.

I woke with a jolt, every nerve tingling. I had no idea what disturbed me but my sleep-addled brain hoped it was a passing maggot. I had chosen our resting place to avoid the drizzle but the striate's deep shade most likely saved us from being slain as we slept.

I did not recognise the Mechs but the moons' light glanced off their weapons and for a sickening moment I thought they were trained on us. Then I realised they pointed to our right. The Mechs whispered and one stifled a giggle and that alone told me he was high on arrash.

It also explained the speed of their travel. Arrash did not just bestow a sense of invincibility; it shot the whole body into overdrive. Addicts could run for days, but when the crash came, it was catastrophic

'The heart can just stop. Bang. No warning,' Joseph had told me, and that if the Fighting had lasted longer, SciCorp might have simply outlasted the Mechs. But the Mechs had weapons and that changed everything.

My heart beat as fast as an addict's must as I watched the Mechs. I was terrified Lirra would wake and betray our presence or they would see us anyway. Then they would laugh as they dispatched us like a couple of maggots.

The Mechs crunched their way forward through the detritus looking straight ahead or they would have seen us, despite the striate's shade. I followed their gaze, relieved and dismayed to see a shadowy procession of maggots moving unhurriedly through the trees.

And then it began. The blasts tore through me as if I had been shot, the ear-splitting volley interspersed with the Mechs' squeals of laughter. Lirra jerked upright and I clamped a restraining hand on her arm but could not drag my eyes from the slaughter.

The Mechs followed the maggots into the trees blasting them as they went and the sweet smell of arrash filled the air. One maggot fell nearby, its delicate webs of skin fluttering before they settled in a shining, motionless heap.

Lirra shook with great wrenching sobs but she made no sound as I held her close. Part of me yammered to slip away deeper in the striate but another part was too shocked to move, and for a few crucial seconds, I hesitated.

This turned out to be very, very lucky for even as the smell of blood joined the smell of sweetness, shadcats emerged from the gloom. If I had believed the day could not get any worse, I was about to be proved wrong.

I had not seen a shadcat since I was a child but they had lost none of their terror. A face like a skull with small flattened ears; curved teeth for ripping flesh; a sparse ginger pelt; and the stink of meat left out in the sun.

Shadcats were smart and opportunistic feeders and it was likely they had learned to associate food with the sound of weapons fire. Some began to gorge on the maggots nearby but the pack leader stared in the direction the Mechs had gone. The firing had stopped but the Mechs' shouts were audible as was their crashing about in the detritus.

The survival rule of staying still drummed into us at Station One and Haven thundered through my brain. Shadcats' sense of hearing and smell were acute but it was movement that drew them. The Mechs' ruckus told me they were coming back but so did the shadcats. They ceased feeding and raised their heads.

The Mechs were oblivious and even within range of the shadcats, their swagger did not change. They still laughed as they fired but shadcats are not maggots. Even a wounded shadcat can kill you before it dies and that was more or less what happened.

We remained motionless through the second round of slaughter, Lirra's face buried deep in my jacket until the shadcats had finished their meal and slunk away.

Even then it was a long time before she raised her head. 'Let us go,' she said hoarsely.

'Not until I get their weapons.'

'We are not like them!' she hissed.

'I want to even up the odds.'

One of the Mech's weapons was still in his hand but his hand was some distance from his body. The other weapon was buried under the remains of a maggot. I wiped the mess off and emptied the Mechs' jackets of ammunition.

I knew how to load the weapons thanks to the holo I watched at Station One, but I still fumbled badly, put off by Lirra's glare. 'You should carry one of them,' I said, as I jammed the weapons into my belt and we set off.

'I do not want to be a Mech even if you do.'

'I never said I wanted to be a Mech.'

'So, you are carrying weapons for decoration, are you?'

Lirra's tone was scathing and my own anger flared. 'I am carrying them so I have some hope of protecting you!'

'Since when was it your job to protect me?' she demanded furiously. 'Or even show any interest in me? I have not noticed you seek my company at Haven lately but suddenly I am your responsibility. Well, you can count me out. I am not going to be your craddy excuse to avenge your father.'

She strode off but I was so taken aback it took me a moment to start after her. She had not gone far. The butchery in the trees was even worse than where we sheltered but she was intent on something in the shadows. I had the weapon in my hand before I realised it was a maggot, in fact, the maggot I had seen twice before.

The maggot was motionless but there was something about the tilt of her head as she stared at me that was like a knife in the guts. I felt as if I had wrought the carnage. I wondered how she had escaped and whether she felt grief for those of her kind that had not. I wondered too whether she could differentiate between SciCorp and Mechs. It was probably even less likely than us differentiating between maggots, I decided grimly.

'Warrain.'

She said my name in the same way as before but I still had no idea what it meant. I came level with Lirra, expecting the maggot to flee but her faceted eyes remained fixed on me.

'What do you want?' I asked, my face warming as if I asked the question of a rock and expected the rock to reply. My only small comfort was I could not possibly sink any lower in Lirra's eyes.

The maggot simply looked back to the shattered bodies of the other maggots. 'It is not safe for you here,' I said slowly, again having no idea whether she understood. 'You should go back to where you came from.'

She looked at me and then up to the sky, the movement of her head almost mechanical and completely unlike the smooth motions of a human or shadcat. Then she stared up the valley and back to me, again in two distinct movements.

'Warrain.'

It was the third time she called me by name but then weapons' fire sounded again, ahead of us this time, between us and Haven.

'How the crad did Mechs get in front?' I demanded, of no one in particular.

'They are on arrash,' said Lirra shortly. 'They won't have slept.'

'Then we won't either,' I said and started forward but Lirra gripped my arm.

'The maggot is asking you for help.'

'She said my name, that is all,' I retorted.

I tried to shrug Lirra off, but her grip tightened. 'Do not play stupid with me, Warrain. Her meaning is clear.'

'We do not have time!'

'For what? To do what SciCorp came here for? To be true to ourselves? To not act like the stinking Mechs?'

'We need to warn Haven!'

'They are not deaf, Warrain. They have been warned!'

With a shrug, the maggot unfurled her delicate webs of skin: a throw of lace veined with black and I was enveloped in the scent of arrash. It was like being speared through the heart with some barbed thing of molten metal. I staggered sideways into Lirra and we had to hold each other up until our heads cleared.

'Was that some sort of bribe?' I gasped.

'Arrash,' mumbled Lirra, 'but she seems barely aware of us.'

Lirra was right. The maggot's attention was fixed on the sky and I had no need to follow her gaze to know she stared at the third moon. Then she looked at me again and there was no mistaking her meaning as she moved off at the same unhurried pace as the other maggots.

The quickest route to Haven lay straight ahead but I gritted my teeth and followed the maggot deeper into the valley. Lirra was right about the weapons fire warning Micah and about my SciCorp obligations but turning away from Haven at that moment was the hardest thing I had ever done. The only compensation was that Lirra followed me.

The maggot made her way deeper into the detritus and disappeared into a maggot hole, and we scrambled in after her. Once inside, the maggot picked up her pace, using both sets of arms as well as her legs in a scuttling gait and we had to jog to keep up.

Our pace gave me no time to check for the fal-lichen that warned of shafts but as we entered the tunnel from solid ground, we would not have far to fall. It would be a different story higher in the Ranges though.

'I have no idea why I am following a craddy maggot,' I panted.

'And I have no idea why I am following you,' said Lirra, still angry with me.

'That makes two of us,' I snapped back. 'Considering how obnoxious you find my company, I thought you would have headed off on your own by now.'

'There does not seem to be any side turnings,' she retorted, 'but when one turns up, be sure I am taking it.'

'That is too risky,' I said, sobering.

'As if you care!'

I rounded on her angrily. 'Of course, I care!'

'How much Warrain? How much do you really care?'

Here it was again; the opportunity to declare my feelings. There was enough lumin-lichen to see the challenge in her face and the thud of my heart had nothing to do with our pace up the tunnel.

Lirra wanted me to say I loved her and I did love her; had loved her from when, as muddy orphans, we worked together on Haven's first rude shelter. But my head was full of the threat to Haven and the maggot's bizarre behaviour and again I hesitated.

'Not enough,' she muttered as she shoved past me, and then the world exploded.

Weapons fire shattered the roof and plunged us into a choking cloud of detritus. The noise was horrendous and I launched myself blindly to where Lirra had been, landed on top of her, and sent us both sprawling.

But thoughts of pulling her to safety vanished in an instant; there was no safety, just luck, or its absence. I covered her body with mine as weapons fire raked the floor but somehow missed, and then the firing stopped.

There was a gaping hole in the roof and in the spill of light, I saw the still shape of the maggot a little ahead. So did the Mechs. Guffawing at their handiwork, they swung themselves down. I reached for my weapon and Lirra caught my wrist. 'No!' she hissed.

The Mechs either sensed her movement or heard her and spun. There was no hesitation from them—from Seth. I had an instant to recognise him, and he me, before I heard the blast.

I did not feel the missile plough into me, just found myself several lengths further down the tunnel, thrown there by the impact. There was no pain either, at first, just fear for Lirra.

I was vaguely aware the other Mech bent over the maggot, his lust for arrash outweighing any concern for me, or perhaps he knew Seth was about to blast me out of existence.

And then Seth filled my line of vision. Arrash amplified his murderous rage as he swaggered towards me. 'Time to discuss my brother,' he slurred.

His mouth curved in a smile to expose his teeth as he planted the weapon between my eyes. He reminded me of shadcat and I was desperately trying to replace the image with something better to carry into death when the blast sounded.

Again, I had no sensation of having been shot or of pain. Seth's eyes widened as if he too were astonished I showed no reaction and then he toppled sideways and lay still. I was still grappling with this anomaly when there was another blast.

I turned my head on the tunnel floor because I could no longer raise it. The other Mech lay prone next to the maggot's body and, as Lirra threw the weapon from her and crouched beside me, I used the last of my strength to say the words I should have said earlier.

'I love you.' Wetness hit my face; Lirra's tears, I realised in wonder.

'Do not die, do not die,' she whispered frantically, but as pain tore through me and the darkness beckoned with its promise of oblivion, I let myself go.

If Seth's aim had not been affected by arrash and arrogance, and Lirra had not been a medico in training, I would have died there on the tunnel floor. Even so, enough of my blood pumped out to make me look more like a white fella than a black one, or so Lirra told me when I came to my senses. It was typical of her to skip over what I later learned was a desperate fight to stop me dying of shock.

Luck was again on my side. This part of the tunnel was rich in otamus and rustico lichens so Lirra not only had the means to stop the bleeding but the moisture to replenish the fluids I lost. The maggot was lucky too for the same reason, although Lirra could do nothing about the damage the Mech inflicted milking her arrash.

It was past midnight before Lirra even let me sit up. She tended the maggot throughout the night and I watched, my head propped against my pack. It was only a maggot, I told myself, like the countless broken and dead ones marking the Mechs' murderous passage but she was not just another maggot. She had called me by name and, in doing so, called upon my help.

But we shared a greater bond than that. The maggot's planet had been invaded by a species that treated them like vermin and the memory of my own peoples' slaughter was imprinted in my DNA and, no matter how I tried to dismiss a connection between us, a link had been forged.

Lirra packed my wound with rustico lichen she replenished as each batch filled with stale blood. The missile had missed bone but made a mess of my muscles and I wondered how much use I would be at Haven if there were a Haven to return to.

The maggot was in worse shape than me; one of her limbs shattered just below the shoulder. Had she been human, the injury would have killed her, but instead, the wound had sealed over and the smashed limb fallen off.

Despite the desperation of our situation, Lirra was excited by the maggot's capacity to heal although the maggot's power did not extend to her torn arrash pouch. Her skin had taken on a translucent sheen, as if her essence drew inwards to protect her vital organs, and I feared she would die anyway.

Lirra had dragged Seth's body and the body of the other Mech, who I did not recognise, to the far side of the tunnel, and torn up their shirts for bandages. She had taken their weapons too and their ammunition and stacked it in a neat pile beside me.

Lirra had acted with ruthless efficiency to save me but I wondered how killing had affected her. I knew the scars killing left and not just on my face, and taking life was the exact opposite of Lirra's passion for healing.

It was not until the moons' light streamed in through the shattered roof that she settled beside me and took my hand. I locked my fingers through hers and she leaned over, careful not to touch my shoulder, and kissed me gently on the mouth.

'I love you, Lirra,' I said.

She gave a lop-sided smile. 'Typical IFNO you had to be shot to admit it.'

'Typical IFNO you have to rub salt into an injured man's wounds,' I retorted.

'Not salt, Warrain, rustico lichen and it seems to have healing properties no one guessed.'

'That is because we had no cause to treat these sort of wounds,' I said.

'No.'

Lirra's smile disappeared and I regretted reminding her of what might lay ahead. 'How is the maggot?' I asked.

'The stump healed so quickly I wonder if they are capable of growing new limbs.'

'Maybe that is what the arrash is for,' I said.

'Perhaps,' said Lirra, 'although before we arrived, you would not think they had much need to repair themselves.'

'Maybe they evolved arrash for the aftermath of shadcat attacks or to repel them,' I said. The theory maggots used arrash defensively like the Earth species skunk used a foul stink was not new, but hard to prove.

Whatever its purpose, its opioid effects on humans put the species at risk well before the Mechs' arrash-fuelled rampage. Joseph had described how some Earth species were wiped out because they had parts resembling male genitals and men believed eating them made them virile.

The pain that throbbed through me was worsened by dread of what the Mechs might be up to at Haven. We had heard no shooting for hours, which meant either the Mechs had fallen into arrash-induced stupors or else Haven was already lost.

The possibility was enough for me to struggle to sit but Lirra's firm hand pushed me back. 'We need to get going,' I gasped.

'If you sleep the rest of the night, we might consider it in the morning.'

'We do not have that luxury.'

'Oh, yes we do, Warrain. We have evened the odds, remember. We can blast them to pieces before they blast us to pieces.'

I wished I had the strength to take her in my arms but as waves of pain beat at me I even struggled to control my breathing. 'I do not even know if … I could … kill again,' I panted. 'I can still feel … what it was like … to strangle Seth's brother and now … Seth is dead too. And … for what? Even … if they take Haven …they will not have the skills to run it.

'You saw … how inept they had become … at Station One. And we would have to … build another Haven … to start again and again in some … endless …violence-fuelled cycle.'

Lirra's hand stroked my face but my throat tightened. Losing Haven meant losing the Infirmary that allowed Haven's women, such as Lirra, to give birth in safety and I gave a shuddering groan.

'Is the pain worse?' she asked.

'No.'

She laughed softly. 'You always were a rotten liar, Warrain.'

'Maybe … I should … practise more.'

'Never do that! Not with me or anyone else. The truth is important.'

'Okay, so . . . let us have it. We cannot afford to stay here . . . not for … the whole night. We need to see . . . what is happening . . . at Haven.' She said nothing and I licked my cracked lips. 'And if . . . there has been fighting . . . they will need . . . your skills.'

Lirra stiffened. 'That was a craddy trick,' she said.

'But … not . . . dishonest,' I managed to say, as the dark started to reclaim me. I sensed her lean over me for my eyes had shut and I did not have the strength to pull them open again.

'It is my fault you were shot,' she said brokenly.

'Not yours,' I gasped. 'None of this ... is your ...' but I could not even finish the sentence.

The pain was less ferocious when I roused and the tunnel filled with dawn's pale sheen. The maggot still stood under the shattered roof and, in the light, her fur gleamed an iridescent blue.

I blinked in astonishment and Lirra's cool hand came to my forehead. 'Is the pain any better?'

'Yes,' I said.

'You never know what lichen will hide,' she murmured, and followed my gaze. 'She has been there all night, just as you see her now.' The maggot turned to us in her usual jerky fashion and her faceted eyes fastened on mine.

'There is no way Warrain can take you anywhere,' said Lirra. The determination in her voice was nothing new but the steely thread of protectiveness was. Even so, I wanted the final say over what I could and could not do.

'We need to get moving,' I said.

Lirra did not argue this time just coated the last of the zitin cakes with a strange mix of lichens and insisted I eat the lot. I did not waste my strength arguing either, just forced the bitter meal down.

She hauled me to my feet and held me until I steadied. I had some of the ammunition in my pockets and two weapons in my belt and Lirra carried the rest of the ammunition and the other two weapons. We did not discuss whether we would use but they were loaded.

The maggot seemed content to stay with us and my mood lifted when I sensed the tunnel swing back in Haven's direction. Daylight sifted through the tunnel's roof to make travelling easier but it meant there was only a single layer of detritus between us and any weapons fire.

I had other things to worry about though like putting one foot in front of the other. I suspected the concoction Lirra fed me had an anesthetising effect but not an energising one and I used a weapon, muzzle to the ground, to help me along.

'It is good they serve some useful purpose,' observed Lirra acidly.

The lack of weapons fire continued to worry me. The Mechs might already be relaxing in their new Station or the battle for Haven yet to begin, then again, the silence might be part of some Mech strategy. I was so taken up with the possibilities I failed to notice the absence of other maggots until Lirra pointed it out.

'You would think there would be others,' she said, 'given they move towards the Ranges and, according to Joseph, made the tunnels in the first place.'

I nodded, having heard Joseph on the topic: a great city of maggot-holes hidden from our eyes, made by maggots for their own secret purposes. 'Maybe there are more in front and following,' I suggested.

'None passed while I treated your shoulder or while you slept and we are hardly moving fast now. Maybe this is a special tunnel that only your friend knows about.'

'Or only she uses,' I added. Lirra looked at me questioningly and I shrugged, something I regretted as pain slashed through my shoulder. 'She is . . . the only female . . . we have seen,' I managed to say, 'and the . . . only blue one.'

'She is not blue exactly.'

'Blue-tinged,' I amended.

'Sex and colour might go together,' said Lirra thoughtfully. 'They might be blueish when they take on female form and brown in male form.'

'And do they learn English at the same time?'

I had not intended to have a dig at Lirra but, despite being the son of scientists, I had never warmed to the scientific view of the world. For one thing, it did not explain my ability to sense things and for another, it confined things in categories and sub-categories and sub-sub-categories that were better left free.

'If the maggot had heard your name before, it could be mimicry,' said Lirra, her brows quirked in thought. 'Given they have an ILFII of six, they should have a communication system. There is no record of them using mimicry though or anything classified as a language.'

'No record we can get our hands on,' I said, made irritable by the pain. Crad! I sounded like Joseph again.

'Possibly. The Explorer Ships sent all sorts of data back to Space Corp to be crunched and repackaged according to what Stations needed to know. Then it was all dispatched in Data Pods for safe-keeping to help humankind impose their wondrous systems upon the universe. I am sure the maggots are appreciative, especially the milked and murdered ones.'

I had never heard Lirra criticise the idea of Sat settlements but she was vitriolic and I wondered if it were delayed shock at having to kill. Her angry eyes came to mine. 'We are doing to the maggots what was done to our ancestors.'

She was clearly distressed and I kept my voice light. 'Not us personally.'

'Humans!' she spat.

'The Protocols—' I began, but Lirra snorted and I decided not to waste my precious strength. We were close to where we had to exit anyway and I staggered to a stop. 'We need to find a way out,' I said, instinctively lowering my voice.

'You know the tunnels, Warrain; how thick are the roofs here?'

Her question took me a back. The usual way out, when there were no exits, was to burrow up through the layers but I was in no state to climb or dig and I cursed under my breath.

'I am not strong enough to climb out,' I admitted.

'And smart enough to realise it,' said Lirra acerbically, 'which is encouraging. We will keep going until we find an exit and then backtrack.'

Lirra being right did nothing to improve my temper. Pain had resumed its searing throb but we did not have to go far before light heralded a break in the wall. The maggot kept going and I called to her to stop.

She did and stared at me impassively. The light illuminated a body robbed of symmetry by the missing limb and of substance by the plundered pouch. She looked as brittle as glass. What she had suffered was akin to rape and memories of my ancestors' suffering renewed my determination to make amends.

'Warrain.'

Her voice was harsher now and even if it were mimicry, it sent shivers down my spine. 'Warrain is in no state to go anywhere,' said Lirra. 'He needs to—'

'We need to check Haven first,' I said to the maggot. 'Then I will go with you.'

'You can barely walk,' hissed Lirra. 'You need proper treatment and rest.'

'Neither of which is likely at Haven,' I said. 'If we still control it, they will need able-bodied men and medicos not more wounded.'

'Warrain—'

'We are doing to the maggots what was done to our ancestors. You said it yourself. If I can help her, I will.'

'And who will help you?' demanded Lirra, close to tears. 'Not some maggot!'

I gently brushed the hair from her eyes. 'Let us see what has happened at Haven first. If it is gone, we will both go where the maggot leads. There might be nowhere else.'

18

I was relieved the maggot stayed in the tunnel. I had no idea how quickly an injured maggot could move and doubted she had the sense to hide. I gripped Lirra's hand as I staggered to the shadow of the closest boulder, slumped behind it, and peered about.

We were in one of the valleys not far above Haven, I saw in relief. The sun had yet to break the horizon but there was plenty of light given the cloud had shredded to reveal the third moon. It was gigantic and so close it obscured the other two. It was also full.

'The tides at Station One must be enormous,' I whispered.

Lirra's hand convulsed in mine. If Station One had gone under, it would not be hate or greed that drove the Mechs in our direction but need. Not that the reason mattered if we were homeless again.

We scrambled from rock-shadow to rock-shadow until we had a clear view of Haven and rested while I struggled to get my pain under control. Haven looked peaceful, as if everyone were asleep or dead. It was early but no one at Haven slept late. My knotted muscles sent fresh knives of pain through my shoulder and I needed no special senses to pick up Lirra's tension.

We crouched in the shadows in an unspoken pact to wait until something happened because the alternative, to confirm those of SciCorp had been murdered, was too terrible to contemplate.

The sun edged above the horizon and an argent-owl swooped by, late to its roost. Sprites started up too, right on cue. At least we were quiet enough for them not to launch alarm calls.

'I could investigate,' said Lirra finally.

'No.'

'I have weapons, remember.'

'And would you use them?'

Her silence was answer enough. The Mech and SciCorp families had endured the long voyage from Earth together and worked in their own ways to create Station One. As a child, I played with Mech children and Lirra had too.

'We will go down together,' I said hoarsely, as pain pulsed with each heartbeat. 'But just close enough … to see … what is going on.'

'Eat this first,' said Lirra, and pulled a handful of strange coloured lichen from her pocket.

I hoped it was for pain but did not bother to ask, just obediently chewed the sour mass, and gulped down the last of the water to rinse the taste from my mouth.

'We will fill the canteens at the next well,' she said, and packed them away.

We set off, slowed by my weakness, and had not gone far when Lirra caught my arm. 'There is a man,' she hissed.

I fumbled for a weapon, appalled I had not noticed him then realised he was prone on the ground. The cress nearby indicated a well and I wondered whether he guarded it or was part of some sort of trap.

'Is he asleep?' whispered Lirra.

'I do not think so.'

I could not see his face but the angle of his body looked strange and we were too far away to tell whether his clothes were Mech or SciCorp. If he were dead, it shortened the odds he was SciCorp and been killed as he fled whereas if he were Mech, he was probably in an arrash-induced stupor.

Men roused quickly from such stupors in vile and violent moods and I readied the weapon. 'You stay here,' I said.

'I know how to shoot as well as you do.'

'Lirra …'

'I watched lots of holos on weaponry on the Settler Ship.' She took a deep breath. 'We are in this together, Warrain, besides, you are in no state to fight.'

'I do not intend to fight,' I said, then realised the alternative was to shoot the Mech as he slept. My stomach turned at the thought.

'We are wasting time,' she said gently.

I hauled myself up and we crept forward. The rise and fall of his chest was clear as was his Mech clothing and sweat trickled down my back. I half hoped he would wake and we would have to shoot him in self-defence but he remained motionless.

Lirra bent and, before I could stop her, tossed a handful of pebbles at him. The warning cry died in my throat but the man did not stir. 'That was lunacy,' I panted, as pain fire-stormed my shoulder.

'His breathing was too low for sleep or arrash,' she said. 'I did not think he—'

I rounded on her furiously. 'That is the problem! You did not think!'

'Warrain—'

'You could have been shot! Do not ever do that again!' I retched and had to plant the weapon in the ground to hold myself up.

'Warrain, you are over-reacting. I am a medico. I could tell from his breathing there was no risk.'

'He might have altered his breathing! He might have had a weapon tucked under him! We could not see his hands!'

'There was no risk,' she repeated, her voice taking on the stubborn edge I knew so well. In the past, I would have let it go but my anger built rather than diminished.

'Give me your word you will not take risks like that again,' I demanded.

'Do not be ridiculous! We are going to Haven and who knows what we will discover there? Do you want me to find some hole to hide in?'

In truth, I did want her to find some hole to hide in, a place beyond the reach of Mech weaponry but I was too infuriated to reply. Lirra bent and brought her face close to the Mech's, then went to the well, sniffed it and gave a low laugh.

'I am glad you find this whole crad-heap amusing,' I growled.

'Not amusing,' she said, 'but very, very encouraging. Haven has drugged the wells.'

'What?'

'The taint is hard to pick up, but I am guessing they used a mixture of bresh and sael lichens. Clever, clever Micah, or more likely, clever Dimitri. It has his chemist's fingerprints all over it.' She was still smiling as she straightened.

The early morning light caught the graceful curve of her cheek and neck, and I decided whichever gods ruled Imago were vindictive. They had revealed the most precious thing in the world at a time I was most likely to lose it.

'Micah would have realised the new moon's tidal implications for Station One,' said Lirra, turning back, 'and have predicted the Mechs would seek a new home on higher ground. It is a two-day journey and the Mechs would have left in a hurry.

'Given the wells along the way, carrying water would not have been a priority but if the Mechs did bring water, they would have been out of it by the time they neared Haven. I am guessing Haven has drugged all the wells within a certain radius. It is a clever tactic.'

'But a short term one. Micah should have poisoned them.'

'And become a mass murderer? That is what the Ancients did to Micah's people in the twentieth century.'

'Kill or be killed,' I said, and remembered not to shrug. 'It is what our ancestors discovered the hard way.'

'I know you do not really believe that,' said Lirra. 'SciCorp is not like that and nor are you.'

'Which is why our ancestors lost their lands; which is why we lost Station One; which is why we are skulking in the shadows, wondering if we will lose Haven.'

'Micah is not skulking,' said Lirra tersely, 'or wasting time on self-pity. He is doing things to ensure the Fighting of five years ago is not repeated.'

I made no reply, busy relieving the Mech of his weapon and ammunition. I removed his belt too and used it along with material from his jacket to bind his hands and feet.

'We cannot just leave him here for shadcats,' said Lirra worriedly.

'Micah will soon fetch him, assuming everything is as pleasant at Haven as you claim.'

'I did not claim anything, Warrain. I just drew conclusions based on the evidence.'

'Like a good little SciCorp medico,' I said sarcastically.

'Like someone tackling what is happening now instead of wallowing in the past! The past is gone Warrain but we have a chance to make something better.'

Lirra reminded me of the holos on the Settler Ship that had been full of inspiring words about carving out new futures and vision of people gazing purposefully off into the distance. No doubt they were meant to encourage Settlers when the awful reality of their one-way ticket to an alien planet sank in. Joseph called the holos propaganda, but I resisted the urge to point this out to Lirra; I had been nasty enough for one day.

In the end we half-dragged, half-carried the Mech behind a boulder. It made him less obvious to roaming shadcats and stopped him serving as a warning to other Mechs. We did not speak again until we neared Haven's boundary of orshron leaves; my silence a result of pain and Lirra's, I suspect, of annoyance with me.

Despite the unconscious Mech, we had no proof who occupied Haven and we used the last of the boulders for a final reconnoitre. Had I just returned from a jaunt high into the Ranges, I would have been in the Gathering Pod by now stuffing myself with zitin cakes, but I had a ragged wound to my shoulder and was possibly about to gain a second fatal one.

At least Lirra would be safe, I consoled myself. As a female and a medico, she was valuable to the Mechs unless they were arrash-addled and mistook her for a man or were simply vindictive.

'I want you to stay here,' I whispered.

'We have had this argument, Warrain. If anything, you should stay here. If the Mechs are in control, they are not likely to kill me but they will certainly kill you. And if I do not return, you can head deeper into the Ranges. It will be where SciCorp survivors have gone.'

'I am not running a second time and I am not abandoning you.'

Her eyes gentled and she ran her fingers down my cheek. 'Stubborn to the end,' she murmured.

I managed to smile but I desperately hoped her words were not prophetic.

19

We left our shelter and came down to the pungent, orshron-strewn perimeter. Haven still looked deserted which seemed increasingly ominous. Surely if SciCorp held Haven, they would have mounted some sort of guard?

We slipped across the yard, keeping to the shadows in the lee of each pod and were near the Infirmary before I realised we had not decided which pod to check first. The same thought seemed to occur to Lirra and we came to a stop and looked at each other. It was a moment of hesitation that cost us dearly.

Even had I not been injured, I could not have fought off multiple attackers and judging by the arms that seized us and expertly stripped us of weapons and ammunition, there were at least three of them.

Hands on the backs of our necks kept our faces turned to the ground and our captors held their silence as they forced us forward across the yard. One of them gripped my injured shoulder and the pain was so ferocious, I failed to wonder why they did not speak.

'He is wounded,' objected Lirra angrily, but it made no difference.

They manhandled us to Micah's pod, hauled us into what had been his office, and the door slammed behind us. Micah sat in his usual position behind his rast-wood desk and the only explanation my pain-befuddled brain could come up with was that he had sold us out.

The Mechs released us and I clutched the edge of the desk to stop myself falling but Lirra whirled to face our attackers. 'Adrian,' she gasped. 'And Hans and Bjorn. But . . . you are dressed as Mechs.'

I managed to straighten, the sweat cold on my face, and Micah was suddenly beside me, easing me into a chair. 'We have set up Haven as if the Mechs are in charge,' he said. 'The Mechs trickling in now think Haven is already in their hands. It has made their capture easier that and our experiment in water enhancement.'

'We noticed that,' said Lirra. 'We left a Mech lying bound further up the valley.'

'He will be retrieved as soon as possible,' said Micah, and paused. It was obvious he was about to deliver bad news and I was reminded of Singh and his wish for peace.

'While our little tricks have made the capture of Mechs easier, they have not been foolproof,' he said. 'The first Mechs arrived quicker than anticipated and arrash-affected, something else I had not foreseen. You have just come from Station One. What has happened there?'

'I have a message from their Commander, Ravi Singh,' I said, and handed over the message pouch.

'Ravi?' said Micah in surprise.

'Lirra will explain,' I said hoarsely. 'I need to get back to the maggot.'

'You are in no state to go anywhere,' objected Lirra. 'If you insist on keeping faith with a maggot, I will go.'

Micah's head snapped up. 'What maggot is this?'

'One in female form that can say Warrain's name and seems to want him with her,' said Lirra.

The atmosphere in the pod swung from tension to excitement. Investigating phenomena such as maggots was why SciCorp had come to Imago in the first place, not to fight for our lives.

'I am going,' I said stubbornly.

I heard Lirra draw breath to argue but Micah spoke first. 'It is Warrain's decision whether he stays or goes, Lirra, but we need you here.'

'You have Thi and Petar,' she retorted.

'Thi is dead and Petar is wounded,' he replied. There was a short silence while Lirra and I digested this shocking fact. 'You and Adrian are the best medicos of those that remain,' continued Micah. 'That Warrain is still on his feet is testament to your skills and if he is able to add to our understanding of the maggots, so much the better.

'In the meantime, Adrian and Hans will escort you to the Infirmary to keep up our little subterfuge but then you must make your farewells. I need you at work, Lirra, before the sun clears the Ranges.'

It was an order, despite being delivered in Micah's usual quiet way. You must make your farewells; the words haunted me as we made our way across the yard, still clearly under Mech guard. Lirra's hand slipped into mine but we did not speak.

'It is good you have brought more weapons and ammunition,' said Adrian, as we walked, 'although Micah will only use them as a last resort. He says we have other weapons and he is right.

'Apart from enhancing the wells, we have put a little enhancement in the canteens of our prisoners. It keeps them placid and, as an added bonus, helps them come down off the arrash.' Adrian grinned. 'But it is still good to have weapons.'

'Where have you put the Mechs?' I asked.

'In one of the couple's pods. It is secure enough for the seven we have so far especially as they are nice and dozy.' He opened the door to the Infirmary. 'I will leave Hans and Bjorn to guard you while I fetch you some food. That way we will meet Micah's deadline.'

Bjorn and Hans ushered us in then withdrew to guard the door. They ensured any watchers saw us as captives and Haven was safely in Mech hands, but it also gave us time alone.

The other trainee medicos were clearly relieved to see Lirra but she only nodded to them as she helped me to a cubicle and sat me down on a pallet. Then she disappeared to collect whatever she needed, leaving me to contemplate the rast room-divider and that this might be the last time we ever saw each other.

It gave me time to think of the right words to make my farewell but I was in pain and so tired I had to force myself not to lie down and sleep. Even when Lirra returned with hot water, clean bandages and more lichens to pack the wound, I could think of nothing to say.

I simply watched her work in the hope her essence seeped into my DNA and remained there with everything else that made me who I was.

She finished and eased me into a clean shirt and still I remained silent. 'No words of farewell, Warrain?' she said, with a smile that failed to reach her eyes.

'I have taken everything I can of you to carry in my heart.'

'There is still room for words,' she said.

I traced her cheek with my good hand. 'You know I love you.'

'Women want to hear it; I want to hear it,' she said, not quite managing to keep the tremor from her voice.

I took a steadying breath. 'I love you, Lirra, and I have always loved you. From the time you trekked away from Station One beside me in your oversized jacket and ugly haircut, to the day you told me I should grow up, to the day I did. I—love—you.'

Her eyes glistened and her mouth came to mine in a gentle kiss. 'And I have always loved you,' she said.

'Lirra—'

A discreet cough sounded from beyond the screen. 'Time to go,' came Adrian's voice.

'I do not want you to go,' said Lirra urgently.

'And I do not want you to stay,' I said, but I did not add any promises I would be back, or we would be together and it would all end happily. I had no idea of the odds of any of these things and Lirra and I had never been into games of pretend. She simply nodded and helped me to my feet.

Adrian waited with Hans and gave a quick outline of how I was to be exited from Haven without arousing suspicion. He and Hans would carry out my dead body and dispose of it like a piece of rubbish.

It was what any arrash-riddled Mech would do with his slain enemy, Adrian told me cheerfully. The only flaw in the plan was if Mechs decided to look for my corpse, but they had no reason to, given that Haven's comforts beckoned.

And so, laughing and hooting, Adrian and Hans carried my limp form up to one of the higher gullies that happened to be not too far from the tunnel where the maggot waited, and deposited me in some bushes.

'I am sorry I grabbed your shoulder,' whispered Adrian, as he crouched beside me. 'I did not realise you were shot.'

'And I am sorry I gave you three days of iza-fungus belly,' I whispered back. 'You were going with Lirra, you see.'

He grinned. 'I see,' he said. 'Stay safe.'

I nodded. 'And you; and keep Lirra safe. She can be headstrong.'

'You are a good pair,' he said, and then he was gone.

Hans flung my pack from a distance and even spat for good measure, and I listened to them singing and shouting as they wove their way back down to Haven. The pack contained food and clean water; more lichen for pain relief; and a loaded weapon and ammunition.

I stayed where I was until the sun was high and when no one appeared, slipped between the boulders back to the tunnel and clambered in. Half of me hoped the maggot had gone but she was where we had left her and I wondered whether she would have died there had I not returned.

Her faceted eyes glimmered as she regarded me, then she moved off down the tunnel and I followed.

The maggot did not go fast, but she went without pause and I swigged from my canteen as I walked. The water's sweetness told me Lirra had added something to shore up my strength or dull the pain or both.

Adrian had loaded my pack with zitin too, which meant if Haven were lost, I had enough food to keep me going until I regrouped with other survivors if there were other survivors. I was grateful to him but hardly reassured.

I concentrated on my breathing to avoid stewing on why I had left Lirra behind to follow a maggot, but my reasons seemed increasingly flimsy. It had been Europa's Ancients who dispossessed my ancestors and the Mechs who wrought the damage on Imago, which made me the descendant of victims and an innocent by-stander, and that meant I owed the maggot nothing.

But my rationalisation rang false. We were as alien to the maggots as the invaders had been to my ancestors and, while some of the invaders had meant my ancestors well, as some of us meant the maggots well, the impact in both cases had been catastrophic.

And then, one day, a maggot had called my name.

Lirra suggested it could simply be mimicry but I sensed there was more to it than that. Like the resonance of a bell that reverberates long after its chime, her calling of me was the echo of a more ancient cry for help. I grimaced as I imagined Lirra's response: Really Warrain, that is more poetry than scientific theory.

The maggot stopped and I jolted from my thoughts. It must be late in the afternoon but the lumin-lichen kept the tunnel's light even, so it was hard to tell. The maggot tilted her head as if she listened and I listened too, heart pounding at the prospect of a storm of weapons fire.

'What is it?' I whispered.

Unsurprisingly the maggot did not answer, instead she clawed at the tunnel wall with her upper limbs. She used a windmill action which would have been effective had her limbs been intact, but her stump was too short to make contact.

'Let me,' I said, but the maggot did not move, and I wedged in beside her. Her stump was on her right side and my left arm too painful to use so, side by side, we formed a single body with one good arm each.

We hacked at the wall in unison and choking detritus filled the air. It did not take long to break into another tunnel but we had not gone far before the maggot decided to repeat the whole, exhausting wall-burrowing thing again.

On and on we toiled, spending as much time burrowing as in travel until, abruptly, we had burrowed out of the tunnels altogether. I wiped the detritus from my eyes and struggled to steady my breathing. We were deep in the Striate Forests and the valley's narrowness told me we were high in the Ranges.

It was windy too, a relief after the tunnels' mustiness, but the wind carried an intense sweetness. My immediate thoughts were of arrash, shattered maggots, and Mechs with weapons, but the scent was subtly different.

Something whirled past my face and I flinched, fearing it was a wrell-wasp, but it was blossom and I gazed about in wonder. The striate was full swirling blossom and it was these creamy star-shaped flowers with their pollen-loaded stamens, that gave the air its honeyed scent.

My hair, jacket and trousers were soon covered in them and they clung to the maggot's fur too. Their sheer volume was astonishing but what shocked me most was that the striate had finally done something.

SciCorp had taken core samples from the detritus in the early days of Station One and dated them to over a hundred Imagoan years and yet, in all the time of Station One's existence, no new layers had been added. The whole forest might have been frozen in time for all the organic activity it showed.

The wind roared through the striates' crowns sending fresh storms of blossom and the ancient trees creaked so much I started to worry more about branches crashing down on our heads than Mech attacks. The wind blew the blossom off us too but as we toiled on up the valley, it was replaced with more in an endless cycle of renewal.

Night fell and as the moons' silvery light pierced the canopy, the blossom fluoresced so that it seemed the trees were filled with stars. Argent-owls swooped through the branches, their metal-bright plumage a flash amongst the blossom, like Creation spirits of the Dreaming. I wished Lirra had been with me to witness this spark of something new, that she and Haven were truly safe, that I was whole and healthy and not riddled with pain.

But wishes were for that boy who had stared down at his old life in Station One intent on revenge, not for the one who wanted to give the maggot something, anything, to compensate for what she had lost.

And it was this new Warrain who pushed on now, not because he knew where he was going, but because he knew there was no going back.

20

I had known the third moon was huge but I was still unprepared for the sight of it when we exited the Striate Forest. It was so big I feared it would collide with Imago rather than swing on past. The possibility was so terrifying it took me a minute to realise the wind was close to gale-force.

I braced myself against a boulder and stared about. The moons' light leant the landscape an eerie sheen, as if the Iron Ranges were lit from within, and then I caught sight of a clefted peak and knew where I was. I had been here as a lost and angry fourteen-year-old boy and again after I murdered Seth's brother. The valley had been deserted then but now it seethed with maggots.

I gaped at them, reminded of a holo on the Settler Ship, of animal mass migrations in Africa in the Ancient days. What had stayed with me was not their sheer numbers, amazing though they were, but that they all headed in the same direction at the same time, as if they were a single organism. It was like that now, the moons silvering the maggots' backs, as they swarmed up the valley.

Exhaustion sucked at my strength and I sagged against the boulder. Why the crad had the maggot wanted me when she had so many of her own kind to keep her company? Maybe it was to act as an anchor, I thought sourly, as the wind buffeted her.

She made no attempt to seek shelter and, even as I watched, was knocked off her feet. She started to roll, propelled along by the wind and I scrambled after her and grabbed a limb. It felt both spongy and brittle and I resisted the urge to snatch my hand back.

I kept a grip on her as we fought our way up the valley. We must have looked like some weird parody of a courting couple, but the feel of her body was not the only thing that set my teeth on edge.

The valley was packed with giant versions of iza-fungus. Their caps were so big I could have used them as seats, those that had not ruptured that is; the ground was strewn with their tattered remains.

I would have preferred to detour round them but that meant climbing the valley's sides and I did not have the strength. I struggled on through them, dragging the maggot behind me. It would have been hard even without being injured and the effort just about finished me off. I yearned to lie down and never get up but there was something about the maggots' relentless push that kept me going too.

The valley narrowed as we neared the peak, funnelling the maggots into ever denser concentrations on the valley floor and then, as if the wind and giant fungi were not crad enough, it started to rain.

Scuds of cloud broke the moonlight into bright flashes and the rain grew until it pelted down. As the small stream on the valley's floor became a torrent, I hauled the maggot to higher ground, having to elbow other maggots aside.

The maggots did not react, even when some of their number fell into the torrent and were swept away. They seemed unaffected by the howling wind and rain too, either that or whatever drove them was more powerful. All that drove me was a desperate need for Lirra, and Haven, and for sweet, sweet sleep.

The maggots headed for the caves, for there was nowhere else, but pain robbed me of wonder at their destination. I wanted to gulp down the concoction Lirra had mixed for me but there was no time.

All I could do was cling to the knowledge the caves were close and I could soon rest. But then something happened that even scoured rest from my mind: a shadcat plummeted from the sky into our midst and tore a maggot apart.

The shock held me frozen and other maggots jostled me as they parted around the remains of their comrade and the feeding shadcat. And then there were dozens of shadcats amongst us snarling and feasting.

I stared up and gasped. They were perched all along the valley sides, letting their meals come to them, I realised numbly and I suddenly recalled something similar in the holo when the migrating animals had crossed a river where ferocious predators lay in wait.

The slaughter had been sickening yet the animals had continued streamed into the water. Survival had been a game of numbers not of individuals and it was the same for the maggots now.

The awfulness of what happened spurred me into action but as I wrenched the maggot further up the valley's side in a last frantic bid to get her to safety, her limb came off in my hand.

I recoiled in disgust, doubled over, and vomited until my belly was empty. The sea of maggots buffeted us as they surged past and I struggled to straighten. The maggot swayed in front of me, her skin translucent as the last of her essence concentrated around the blue pulsing globe of her heart.

She was dying, not in one foul swoop like I would, but layer by layer.

The shock of understanding was akin to being shot a second time. I threw off my pack, picked her up, and ran. I ignored the screaming pain in my shoulder, dodged maggots and shadcats, swerved through the slimed remnants of fungus and, when the valley floor turned to water, leapt from boulder to boulder.

The ragged openings of the caves loomed ahead but as I launched myself up the last of the slope, my feet went from under me and I sprawled headlong over the water-slicked stones. The impact smashed the air from my lungs and sent the maggot sliding into an opening.

She did not rasp out my name or turn her head and nor did I expect it. I clawed my way upright and sobbing with pain, fought my way back through the seething mass, up to a shelf of land just below the peak, and collapsed on my back.

I did not even have the strength to roll onto my belly, just threw my arm over my nose and mouth to block the rain, and let the darkness take me.

It was pain that returned first, followed by the chill discomfort of wet clothes. The sky arched over me in a delicate wash of silvery blue that told me it was dawn again and sprites whistled their warnings.

There was a dull roar too and I managed to pull myself onto my knees. The pain in my shoulder was nauseating and I half considered climbing back down to search for my pack but it was beyond me. Instead I crawled to the top of the ridge and peered over, and what I saw remains burned into my memory to this very day.

A great surge of ocean rolled up the valleys, turning spurs into promontories and drowning all else. Even the mighty spurs that divided Sapphire, Turquoise and Amethyst Bays were reduced to the splayed fingers of a giant hand, grey against the ocean's blue. Station One was gone and I was terrified Haven would follow, even though common sense told me the sea would have to cover all of Imago to take it.

The roar grew as the mighty wave rolled inexorably towards me, obliterating the Striate Forests and wiping out the tunnels. I wondered whether it would reach the caves and drown the maggot and her kind as they sheltered inside and, even as the thought crossed my mind, I sensed movement.

I had the wild idea the maggots had joined me on my perch but if it were a shadcat or Mech, I was already dead. I turned slowly, half expecting a searing bolt to fling me down to be swallowed by the sea, but there was nothing there.

And then, above the water's roar, I heard the rattle of dead leaves or of people whispering. The hair stirred on the back of my neck but I could still see nothing. A storm of flapping sounded from the caves and my heart kicked into overdrive but I told myself the maggots' intrusion had probably disturbed a colony of ghost-bats.

My calmness lasted precisely a moment because a plume of smoke streamed from the cleft above me. At first, I thought the peak was erupting, despite knowing Imago was not volcanic, and then I realised it was not smoke but butterflies.

Thousands of them poured into the sky, flashing gold as their wings caught the first rays of the early morning sun and there, amongst the gold, was a single blue, soaring higher than the rest.

As far as the eye could see, all along the coast, plumes rose from the peaks like the beacons the Ancients used to warn of war, but instead of signalling destruction, Imago's beacons heralded renewal.

Tears streamed down my face as at last I understood what the maggots were, what she was. The planet's name made sense now too, but the human-maggot form was not the imago, the last manifestation of the planet's sentient life-form; this was; these wondrous brown-gold males and iridescent blue female that ensured the next generation came.

The shells I had crunched over on my first visit were the carapaces of their ancestors and, as I had fled with her in that last desperate sprint, she had already been transforming into something that transcended her humanoid state; something that would soar along with the rest of her kind above Imago's soft grey mountains and glittering seas.

It was only later I learned how the striate blossom was carried on the maggots' silken fur up through the valleys, pollinating the striate as they passed; of how the striate seed set in just a few hours so that when the oceans swept the striate forests and detritus away, they left behind lacy blankets of seed-mixed foam, in valleys scoured clean and ready to start the cycle all over again.

The iza-fungus was part of it too, its webs of mycelium stretching under all of Imago's soil and poisoning the sour, sealed earth under Station One but, along with the third moon, triggering the transformation of the striate in the valleys, and coming into a full glorious blossom of giant fungal caps, even as the striate blossomed too.

But I knew none of these things as I stared down at a world made new.

21

If the records in the Data Pod are correct, I will not live to see these momentous events again. The intervals between the risings of the flightborn can exceed a hundred Imagoan years because the third moon, apparently named Artemis after some Ancient god, has a highly elliptical orbit.

It would have been useful to have known all this before Artemis spun into the sky and changed everything, but it took that massive wave of water to finally deliver the Data Pod to us.

No one knows where it had lain in the years since its mistimed entry into Imago's atmosphere, but the wave found it and swept it up almost to Haven's doorstep. Like the Ancients surfing, is how Micah described it, although the Christians were more inclined to think of the Ark. Their praying became fervent for a couple of years but has settled down now.

Whether it was divine intervention or blind luck, it made Joseph a happy man, at least for a while. I helped him sift through the Pod's contents, but once we finished, we spent little time on the data stored there.

It was the story of Earth and of the planet Imago seen through the eyes of those who still lived on Earth and, what I finally understood, is that you cannot make a future based on a foreign past.

Even so, the Data Pod remains valuable. It tells us what we were and why we came to Imago and as an IFNO, I have long understood the need to know that. My blood still quickens when I watch the swirl of stars and sometimes, between waking and sleeping, I can smell the scent of eucalyptus leaves burning in the old way.

It remains part of what I am in my present Dreaming too, and part of what our son is, and his brother or sister, still curled safely in Lirra's belly.

I have added a wealth of records to the Data Pod since and continue to ensure our discoveries of Imago's ways are properly preserved, for I have taken on the role of record keeper. Joseph is pleased but I suspect not surprised; it is the reason he took the trouble to have me with him when I was young, and angry, and only intent on revenge.

The maggots' story is embedded in the records I collate, and SciCorp's and the Mechs', not that we use these terms much anymore. The maggots are more properly called the flightborn in any case, which better fits my last glorious vision of them.

Nothing was salvaged from Station One, which many of SciCorp still regret, but it is difficult to pick and choose what you can take from the past.

Singh was killed in the fighting but Fernandez had the wit to lead most of the women and children to higher ground, and the Mechs not affected by arrash followed. Lirra's mother and brothers were lost, for Pindan would not leave Jacob and, like the other Mechs who had plundered the maggots, he was in a world where wings were common and he could simply rise above the water.

Micah welcomed the surviving Mechs and left it up to them whether they remained in Haven or built another Station near the ruins of the old one but on higher ground. The only condition he imposed was that all weapons and ammunition be destroyed.

You can kill a man with a matra blade or with your bare hands, as I proved, so the great burning we had was more symbolic than anything else. It did not take long for the younger members of Haven and Station One to adapt to each other's company.

Haven's young men welcomed the arrival of the young women from Station One and even the younger Mechs were not averse to a greater choice of partners, despite having to wait a few years. The older men like Fernandez were warier but also pragmatic. Station One was gone and with it, the arrash-fuelled violence that proved so destructive.

Haven was a functioning Station but there were plenty of ways the Mechs could improve it and Haven provided a place where they could work alongside SciCorp to create something better, more Imagoan, according to Lirra, than each could create on their own.

As time has gone on, this has changed too. Mechs with an interest in science are training under the guidance of SciCorp and the SciCorp young keen to fashion the tools and equipment that Haven needs, have skilled men and women keen to teach them. Memories of the old divisions have faded along with our memories of Earth. We are of Imago now, and that is enough.

END OF THE THIRD MOON

I hope you enjoyed The Third Moon. **Authors need reviews!** It's how our readers find us. I would love you to leave me an honest review on Amazon, Goodreads or another of your favourite reader sites. Enjoy free short stories? Visit my website, sign up for my newsletter, and read The Gift and The Tale of Prince Anura.

Works by K S Nikakis

Available on Amazon KDP and a range of digital platforms

Non Fiction

Journey: Seeking the Sacred, Spirit and Soul in the Australian Wilderness – *For fans of Joseph Campbell's hero journey*

When we set out into the wilderness, what is it we really seek?

Do we seek new sights or do we seek new selves? And are we really on one journey or on two?

Journeying fifteen thousand kilometres into Australia's blood-red heart, Nikakis discovers that every journey is perilous, for travellers risk carrying the clutter of their outer lives with them; a clutter that blinds them to the other journey they crave; that of the inner soul-journey into a deeper understanding of self.

To enter Australia's vast Outback wilderness, is to enter a place of endless horizons; a place doused with brilliant gold dawns and dazzling sunsets; a place silvered by star-encrusted night skies and, most importantly, a place of hidden sacred places in whose deep stillness our inner journeys can at last unfold.

In the spirit of travellers like Robert Macfarlane and Scott Stillman, Nikakis asks what it is we really see, feel and understand when we follow in the steps of those who have gone before us deep into the wilderness.

Drawing on her Ph.D. in Joseph Campbell's hero myth, and using original poetry and novel extracts, Nikakis takes us on this second journey; a journey of the sacred, spirit and soul, where our inner selves finally have the time and space to gift us richer and more fully-realised lives.

Fantasy Novel Series

Angel Caste 5 Book Series – available complete in one book or as five individual books: Angel Blood, Angel Breath, Angel Bone, Angel Bound, Angel Blessed.

Angel Caste – Complete 5 Book Series – *A modern female hero on a timeless quest*

A troubled half-angel, a beautiful angel guide, a binding promise . . .

Viv is on day release from jail to attend the funeral of the thug she thinks is her father, when she comes face to face with her real father, the powerful angel Archae Kald. If finding out she's a half-angel isn't shocking enough, Viv discovers her mother isn't dead after all but lost somewhere in the tangle of worlds called the Rynth.

Determined to find the only person who has ever truly loved her, Viv transits to Kald's angel world where he appoints the beautiful Thris as her guide. Thris is kind and caring, unlike the males Viv has known before, but after living on the streets, Viv finds it impossible to trust.

Friendship grows as Thris trains her to travel the rifts, but the Rynth is a dark and dangerous place, even for angels and, as Thris grows increasingly tempted by Viv's emerging angel traits, disaster strikes.

Viv journeys on alone and stumbles into a war zone where she finds a lost child, who she pledges to take to safety but, as the war rages on, deciding who is friend and who is enemy becomes a deadly game of chance.

Bound by his promise to guide Viv to her mother, Thris embarks on a desperate search for her, but a greater threat confronts them both and, in the end, they must fight not just for their own lives, but for the lives of those they love.

The Kira Chronicles 6 Book Series - available complete in one book or as six individual books: The Whisper of Leaves, The Silence of Stone, The Secrets of Stars, The Thunder of Hoofs, The Crying of Birds, The Music of Home.

The Kira Chronicles – Complete 6 Book Series *– traditional fantasy with deep forests and high stakes*

A gold-eyed Healer, a prophecy, two brothers at war.

In seasons long past, twin gold-eyed princes sundered a kingdom. Rejecting his brother Terak's warrior ways, Kasheron led his people deep into the great southern forests and established the healing settlement of Allogrenia. The Tremen flourished, upholding Kasheron's legacy of peace and healing, and protected by the vast, trackless trees.

All Tremen delight in the healing arts, but Kira is the greatest Healer of them all.

To the north of Allogrenia, drought ravages the Shargh's land and, as their suffering escalates, the chief's younger brother seizes on an ancient prophecy to snatch the chiefship for himself. The prophecy links the Shargh's doom to a gold-eyed Healer, and Kira has gold eyes.

The Shargh attack with devastating consequences and Kira must fight to save the wounded, but the Shargh wounds rot, no matter her skill, and Kira finds herself in a deadly race against time. As the slaughter continues, she makes the horrifying discovery that the Shargh hunt her. To halt the attacks and save her people, she sets off for the North to seek aid from her long-sundered warrior kin.

But the dangers beyond the forests exceed even the Shargh attacks. The Tremen detest their warrior kin but Terak's descendants have inflicted a worse fate on the Tremen. Kira's new-found love is torn apart by ancient hostilities and when trust turns to betrayal, it risks everything she has fought for.

As the battles rage on, Kira becomes increasingly sickened by the bloodshed and, desperate to end the suffering once and for all, she sets out on a quest that could cost her everything and everyone she loves.

Fantasy Novels

The Emerald Serpent – *the Celtic Fae in a fight for survival*
Book trailer: https://www.youtube.com/watch?v=bGpKxnpCEMg

Betrayal, torture, death: Etaine lives on only to destroy those who robbed her of everything she loved.

Seven years before, Etaine met a fellow Ranger, Cormac, the he-Eadar she believed was her longed for true-mate. Emerald-eyed, white-skinned, and black-haired, the Eadar had formed Ranger bands to fight the Fada, invading religious zealots determined to replace the Eadar's Serpent Goddess with their own gods of stone.

The pure blood of the ancient Eadar runs strong in Etaine and Cormac's veins, and their joining had the potential to open the Emerald and Serpent Ways to them, old worlds only true-Eadar can enter, but their love affair goes tragically amiss, with catastrophic consequences.

Etaine flees and as the years pass, slowly rebuilds her life, but the Fada attacks grow ever more ferocious, and the Eadar are forced to fight for their very existence. When the Fada mass to commit yet more bloody slaughter and the bands join in a final, desperate effort to defeat them, Etaine comes under Cormac's command, the very last Eadar she wants to see again.

Together they have a weapon that can destroy the Fada, but to use it, Etaine must learn to trust again and Cormac to Remember.

And time runs short: the Serpent rises.

Heart Hunter – *a female hunter on an impossible quest*

Fleet is a young Sceadu hunter: skilled, strong, and fast. She hunts deep into the icy mountains, seeking meat for her people, for the rains have failed and plunged the Sceaudu into hunger.

Her hunts are hard, but she has much to look forward to. Soon she will be gifted her air-name by the Sceadu's shaman, and then she will be a full adult, and free to marry the man she loves.

But while Fleet is on hunt, the old shaman dies, and the new shaman visions a very different future for her: cross the frozen, ice-locked mountains and complete a perilous quest or lose the man she loves forever.

In a moment of anger and frustration, Fleet commits a terrible wrong and sets out into the frigid mountains to atone with her life. In a journey that takes her deep into the earth's darkest places, into strange new worlds, and even into Death itself, she discovers that only she can save her people. To survive, she must draw on every shred of her hunter strength, and doing the impossible, it turns out, is just the beginning.

Messenger – *a dystopic future filled with hope*

In a world made deaf by hatred, who will hear the messenger?

Severine's world ends the day her family is murdered. Being raised in the loving community of gay Travelers always marked her as an outsider, but being female puts her in mortal danger. Women are scarce, precious, and hunted.

When chance brings Severine face to face with the father she has never known, he assigns the son of his murdered best friend to guard her. They soon clash. Severine believes all men are violent brutes and Jeph resents his freedoms being curtailed.

An uneasy understanding grows but Jeph is glad to deliver her to the Enclaves, a sanctuary her father has carved out in the mountains for his women and children. But there is no safety in a world broken by war and sickness and when violence follows her, Severine flees to the northern city of Andhaka in search of a home amongst her mother's people. Jeph follows, bound by loyalty to her father, but the north holds terrible dangers for him.

It's been years since Andhaka has welcomed outsiders with anything but bullets, and to survive and to protect Jeph, Severine must learn to use her enemies' weapons against them. As the stakes rise, she comes to understand the horror of her mother's loss, and what drove her father north seventeen years before. His quest becomes her quest, but she hasn't counted on the savage legacy that war and sickness have left behind, or on falling in love.

I Heard the Wolf Call My Name – *gender-fluid shifters in search of home*

Finalist Best YA Novel – 2019 Aurealis Awards

Jax is just twelve years old and in bird-form high above his island home, when it explodes, killing everyone on it. Believing himself to be the only survivor, he is shocked to come face to face with his boyhood friend, Matiu, ten years later.

Matiu is military and the military needs shifters for a crucial mission, but Jax refuses. Having spent ten long years burying his bizarre shifter past, he isn't about to resurrect it. But Matiu rouses other feelings too that Jax finds harder to ignore.

As the military ramps up pressure to force Jax's cooperation, he shifts to bird-form and flees to the last remaining island, where he crashes in the middle of Anahera's vision-quest.

She searches for her skin-spirit animal to transform her into Ikaika, a protector of her people. She dreams of finding the white-wolf but finds Jax instead and to save him, she must abandon her quest.

Her kindness only adds to Jax's turmoil. To decide who he truly is and where he really belongs, he must first confront his painful past but that isn't the worst of his problems. The forces that blew Jax's island out of existence threaten Anahera's as well, and he might be the only shifter who can save it. But time is running out.

Fantasy Short Stories

The Gift – A Deep Fantasy Short Story #1 – free on my website at www.ksnikakis.com

Excerpt:

Thariel sat for a long time, surveying all around her, as if she ate the world that would soon be memory. Then she took the harness from the mare, and with soft words, thanked her and bade her farewell. Her own feet she turned towards the forest, tossing her face-plate aside as she went, so that her hair fell loose to her waist, then she discarded her chest-armour, the sword and dagger, her bow and quiver.

The trees closed in and she came at last to the lake Men call Menios and stood for a while on its shore. An owl cried and a mouse shrieked, and all around her the souls of the newly dead jostled in their journey to the void.

She stepped into the water and the new life inside her quivered. 'Fear not, little one,' she whispered, in her own tongue. 'We are going home.'

The Tale of Prince Anura – A Deep Fantasy Short Story #2 – free on my website at www.ksnikakis.com

Excerpt:

I should have been happy, for she was beautiful. Dark rivers of curls, skin as white as moonlight on water, breasts softer than spawn, and she loved me well. But her chamber was small, no matter the comfort of her bed, and the old feelings of entrapment rose, as persistent as gas that bubbles from rot below still waters.

I sat at the casement and listened, as I had once loitered near the watery skin of the second world and waited. The moon grew large and small many times, but it came at last, as I knew it would. The soft lament on the night-time air, the song of a soul as confined as mine. It took me a journey of many days through the depths of a massive forest to find her tower.

Stone it was and sheer, and as remote as the third world's glimmer had once been. I sang to her and she answered with sweet melodies of her own and we made love as frogs do, with our voices. And when trust had built, she let down her shining ladder of golden hair.

Glass-Heart – A Deep Fantasy Short Story #3
Finalist Best YA Short Story – 2019 Aurealis Awards

Excerpt:

Geth moved amongst his band, exchanging quiet words while they waited. Some he had fought with since the Tallon's foul ships had first found their shores while others had come later, when the burn of cot and kin had sent them from their valleys.

Hate drove them but hate was no shield against arrow and knife. It was fighting skills that kept them hale, and Geth ensured they had them aplenty. He needed them living, not just for their own sakes and his, but for what would come later. When the Tallon's stain had been scoured away, the destroyed must be rebuilt.

Kyth sat alone and he went to her and gazed about. 'The glass-heart's fled, has it?'

'I sent her to a place of safety. She will come to me when it is over.'

'Safety was what I wanted for you!'

'And what I wanted for Nyar.' Her eyes caught the star-sheen as she looked up at him. 'But you can't always have what you want, can you, Ceannasai?'

Dragon Sprite – A Deep Fantasy Short Story #4

Excerpt:

Genn rocketed straight upwards, not just because she enjoyed seeing the limitless blue sky before her, but because a Waiwin's wing shape made vertical flight harder for them. Orin didn't try to catch her but swept in circles around her, gaining height in an ever-narrowing spiral. It was a clever tactic and one Genn didn't believe he had thought of in the instant she had cleared the trees. He had obviously studied her strategies and developed a plan to counter them or so he thought.

Genn waited until the spiral narrowed to axeel, the minimum distance a Waiwin must keep from a Velven unless she accepted him, then swerved towards him, narrowing the distance between them. Orin's eyes flashed to black, shocked she had accepted him, but before he could act, she folded her wings and dropped.

The strength that had driven Orin's pursuit had surged to his wing-tendrils in anticipation of locking them with hers and he would struggle even to stay airborne until it flowed back.